The Eternal Circle

The Keeper of Ages, Volume 1

Catherine J Rosser

Published by Catherine J Rosser, 2024.

This is a work of fiction. Similarities to real people, places, or events are entirely coincidental.

THE ETERNAL CIRCLE

First edition. October 28, 2024.

Copyright © 2024 Catherine J Rosser.

ISBN: 979-8227545756

Written by Catherine J Rosser.

Table of Contents

The Eternal Circle (The Keeper of Ages, #1) 1
Chapter 1: The Quiet Healer 7
Chapter 2: Echoes of the Past 15
Chapter 3: The Gathering Shadows 23
Chapter 4: The Weight of Immortality 31
Chapter 5: The Awakening of Power 39
Chapter 6: After the Storm 45
Chapter 7: The Road to the Sanctuaries 51
Chapter 8: The Path to the North 55
Chapter 9: Into the Depths of Fear 63
Chapter 10: The Sanctuary's Secret 69
Chapter 11: A Fragile Victory 77
Chapter 12: The Path of Sacrifice 85
Chapter 13: The Weight of Destiny 95
Chapter 14: The Echo of Her Power 103

To the Magic Within All of Us.

Prologue: The Gift of Ages

Long before the rise of empires, when the old gods still walked the earth, the world was a place of boundless magic. The mountains whispered ancient secrets to the wind, the rivers ran with the laughter of forgotten spirits, and the trees stretched toward the sky with the wisdom of millennia in their roots. In those days, the earth was alive in ways that mortals no longer remembered—pulsing with power, every stone and leaf infused with the magic of creation.

It was in this world that **Elora** was born, the youngest daughter of a priestess sworn to the old gods. Her people lived in harmony with the land, drawing strength from the earth and the elements. They knew the language of the wind, the songs of the trees, and the healing power of the plants that grew in the wilds. Elora's mother, **Siril**, was a guardian of these ancient secrets, a woman revered for her connection to the natural world and her ability to heal the sick and wounded.

Elora had inherited her mother's gifts, but even as a child, there was something different about her. The land itself seemed to respond to her in ways it did not with others. When she walked barefoot through the meadows, the grass would bend toward her, as if seeking her touch. The birds would quiet their songs in her presence, only to resume them in perfect harmony with her voice. And the trees—those ancient sentinels of the earth—whispered her name in their rustling leaves, as though they recognized something in her that no one else could.

"Why do the trees speak to me, Mother?" she asked one day, as they gathered herbs in the forest. Her mother smiled softly, her eyes full of both love and quiet mystery.

"They know who you are, my child," Siril replied, her voice like the wind through the leaves. "They sense your connection to the earth. You are more than you know."

As Elora grew, her connection to the natural world deepened. She learned the language of the plants—their whispers telling her of their healing properties, their strengths and weaknesses. She spoke to the animals, understanding their needs and their pain. And she could feel the pulse of the earth beneath her feet, a constant, steady rhythm that matched the beating of her own heart.

Yet, for all the beauty and magic of the world she had known, change was coming. The gods, who had once been so present in the lives of mortals, began to withdraw. The great temples of the gods were abandoned, their sacred fires extinguished. The voices of the earth grew quieter, the magic that had once been everywhere now only flickering in the hidden corners of the world.

One evening, as the sun set in a blaze of gold and crimson over the distant mountains, Siril brought Elora to the sacred grove. It was a place where the veil between the mortal world and the realm of the gods was thin, a place where magic still thrived. The air was thick with the scent of wildflowers and damp earth, and the towering oak trees seemed to hum with ancient power.

Elora knelt beside her mother in the center of the grove, feeling the weight of something vast and eternal pressing in around her. She had always known that her family's connection to the gods was special, but tonight, she sensed that something far greater was at play.

THE ETERNAL CIRCLE

"Why have you brought me here?" Elora asked, her voice barely above a whisper.

Siril took her daughter's hands in her own, her gaze steady and filled with a sadness Elora had never seen before. "The world is changing, my child. The gods are leaving, fading from this realm. Soon, they will no longer walk among us."

Elora's heart tightened. "But why? Why are they abandoning us?"

"It is not abandonment," Siril said softly. "It is the way of things. Even the gods are bound by the cycles of time. They came to this world when it was new, and now their time is ending. But the magic of the earth will remain, as long as there are those who remember."

Elora's gaze drifted to the trees, the ancient oaks that had stood in this grove for longer than any mortal memory. "And what will become of us? What will become of me?"

Her mother hesitated, and in that moment, Elora knew that her mother had brought her here not just to witness the end of an age, but to take on a burden that she could scarcely comprehend.

"The gods have chosen you, Elora," Siril said at last, her voice trembling with emotion. "You are to be their last gift to this world. A keeper of their magic, a guardian of the old ways. You will not fade with time as we do. You will live, ageless, as long as the earth endures."

Elora's breath caught in her throat, her heart pounding in her chest. "What do you mean?"

Siril squeezed her daughter's hands, tears welling in her eyes. "You will live beyond the span of mortals. You will walk the earth for centuries, watching over it, protecting its magic.

You will teach those who seek the old ways, and when the time comes, you will move on, always in silence, always in shadow."

Elora pulled her hands from her mother's grasp, shaking her head in disbelief. "But I don't want this. I don't want to live forever. I don't want to be alone."

Siril's expression softened, her sorrow palpable. "You will not be alone, my daughter. You will have the earth, the sky, the wind, and the trees. And you will meet others like you—beings of magic and power who will walk beside you for a time. But you must understand—this is not a curse. It is a gift. The greatest gift the gods can bestow."

Elora stood, her heart pounding with fear and confusion. The thought of living through centuries, of watching everything she loved fade into memory, was unbearable. "Why me?"

Siril rose to her feet and embraced her daughter tightly. "Because you were born with a heart that listens to the earth, with a soul that carries the strength of the old ways. The gods have seen this in you, and they have chosen you to carry their legacy."

In that moment, the sky above them darkened, the air growing thick with energy. Elora felt it—a presence, vast and powerful, filling the grove. She heard the voice of the earth, a low, deep hum that resonated in her bones. The gods were here, not in form but in spirit, their magic surrounding her, wrapping around her like a cloak.

Elora's body trembled as the power of the old gods flowed into her, filling her with ancient knowledge, with the language of the plants, the animals, the very earth itself. It was overwhelming, terrifying, and beautiful all at once. She felt herself change, her mortal tether loosening as the gift of immortality took root inside her.

And then, as quickly as it had come, the presence was gone. The grove was silent once more, but Elora was no longer the same.

Her mother stepped back, her eyes filled with both pride and sorrow. "You are now the keeper of the old ways, Elora. You are eternal."

Elora looked down at her hands, hands that would never age, never wither. She felt the weight of the world pressing in around her, the responsibility of her new existence settling over her like a heavy mantle.

"I will carry this gift," she whispered, though her heart ached with the loss of the life she had known.

Siril smiled, though her tears fell freely. "The gods have entrusted you with their magic. You will honor them. And you will find peace in the earth, in the world you will protect."

Elora nodded, though her future seemed impossibly vast and uncertain.

As they left the grove that night, Elora knew that her path was now set. She would walk the earth for centuries, learning the language of the land, guiding those who sought her wisdom, and always, always moving forward. She would be many things to many people—healer, teacher, protector—but never would she reveal the full extent of her power.

For she was more than just a healer. She was the last gift of the old gods.

And her journey had only just begun.

Chapter 1: The Quiet Healer

The morning light was soft, golden tendrils stretching lazily across the village. Dew clung to the leaves, glistening like tiny jewels as the sun began its slow ascent over the mountains. Birds filled the air with their songs, their voices harmonizing with the gentle rustle of leaves in the breeze. It was the kind of day that felt timeless, untouched by the march of years, a peaceful oasis in the chaotic churn of the outside world.

Elora stood at the edge of the forest, her bare feet sinking into the cool, damp earth. The forest greeted her like an old friend, its magic wrapping around her like a familiar embrace. She inhaled deeply, taking in the scents of pine, wildflowers, and the subtle earthy musk that always accompanied the break of dawn. For the people of the village, this place was just another forest—a place to gather wood, hunt game, and occasionally seek out her remedies. But to Elora, the forest was alive in a way few could comprehend. It whispered to her, its language ancient and filled with secrets that had long since been forgotten by mortal ears.

She had been here for nearly twenty years now. Long enough for the villagers to grow used to her presence, for the children she had once healed as babies to now have children of their own. And long enough for the quiet whispers to begin. The same whispers she had heard in countless other places over the centuries: *She hasn't aged a day. What kind of magic does she wield? Who is she really?*

Elora ran her fingers over the leaves of a nearby plant, feeling the pulse of life within it, the soft hum of magic that vibrated through the forest. It had always been this way—ever since she was a child. The plants, the animals, even the wind—they all spoke to her in ways that defied the understanding of most mortals. And it was through these quiet conversations that she had learned the art of healing, a gift she had passed down to others countless times.

As she moved through the forest, her steps light and deliberate, her mind drifted to the future. It was almost time to leave. She could feel it, the same way one feels the shift in the air before a storm. The villagers had begun to notice, begun to ask questions. She had seen the way Mira, her apprentice, looked at her sometimes—confusion and curiosity mingling in her young eyes. It wouldn't be long before those questions turned into something more dangerous. Something Elora couldn't afford to confront.

Her pace slowed as she reached a small clearing. At its center stood a simple stone cottage, nestled among the wildflowers and ivy that seemed to thrive in the magical energy surrounding the place. Smoke curled lazily from the chimney, carrying with it the scent of herbs and warm, freshly baked bread.

Mira would be inside, diligently working on her latest task. Elora had been training her for years now, teaching her the ways of the earth, the language of plants, and the art of healing.

Mira was a fast learner, quick with her hands and even quicker with her mind. But there was still so much she didn't know—so much that Elora couldn't tell her.

The door creaked softly as Elora pushed it open, stepping into the warm, herb-scented interior. Mira sat at the small wooden table in the center of the room, grinding dried leaves into a fine powder with a stone pestle. She looked up as Elora entered, her face breaking into a bright, welcoming smile.

"Elora! I was just finishing the poultice for Old Man Jorin," Mira said, holding up the small bundle of herbs wrapped in cloth. "His leg's been bothering him again. Too much time spent in the fields, I think."

Elora smiled, her heart warming at the sight of her apprentice's eager face. "You've done well, Mira. That should help with the swelling."

Mira's smile widened, but there was something else in her eyes—a flicker of worry, of uncertainty. Elora knew what it was. She had seen that same look in countless apprentices over the centuries, the look of someone beginning to realize that their mentor was not like them. That their mentor was something... more.

"Elora," Mira began, her voice hesitant. "There's something I've been meaning to ask you."

Elora's heart sank. Here it was. The beginning of the questions. She had been dreading this moment, but she knew it was inevitable.

"What is it, Mira?" Elora asked gently, though she already knew what the question would be.

Mira set the pestle down, her brow furrowing as she searched for the right words. "It's just... you've been here for as long as I can remember. My mother used to tell stories about you from when she was young. And you haven't changed. Not at all. How is that possible?"

Elora's smile faltered, the weight of her centuries pressing down on her. She had always known this day would come. It always did. The truth of her agelessness could only stay hidden for so long before people began to notice, began to wonder.

"Mira..." Elora began, choosing her words carefully. "There are some things in this world that can't be explained easily. Some things that are part of the old ways—the ways that most people have forgotten."

Mira's eyes widened, a mixture of curiosity and fear flickering across her face. "The old ways? You mean magic?"

Elora nodded slowly. "Yes. Magic. But not the kind of magic you hear about in stories. This is deeper, older. It's tied to the earth, to the very essence of life itself."

Mira leaned forward, her voice barely a whisper. "Is that why you haven't aged?"

Elora hesitated. How could she explain something she barely understood herself? How could she explain the gift—and the burden—that had been placed on her so long ago? The gift of immortality, the power of the old gods, the responsibility she carried to protect the earth and its magic?

"Yes," Elora said softly. "In a way. I was given a gift, long ago. A gift from the old gods. But it's not a gift without its price."

Mira's eyes shone with awe, but there was something else there too—something darker. "So... you can never die?"

Elora looked away, her gaze drifting to the window where the sunlight filtered through the trees, casting long shadows across the floor. "No. I can't."

For a long moment, neither of them spoke. The weight of Elora's words hung in the air, thick and heavy. Mira, for all her youth and inexperience, was beginning to understand. She was beginning to see the burden that Elora carried, the weight of centuries spent moving from place to place, watching the people she cared for grow old and die while she remained unchanged.

"I'm going to have to leave soon," Elora said finally, her voice barely above a whisper.

Mira's head snapped up, her eyes wide with disbelief. "What? But why? You can't leave! The village needs you!"

Elora shook her head sadly. "The village will be fine, Mira. You've learned everything you need to know. You'll take my place."

Mira's face crumpled in confusion and hurt. "But I'm not ready. I—I still need you."

Elora placed a gentle hand on Mira's shoulder, her heart aching for the young woman who had come to mean so much to her. "You are ready, Mira. You've grown into a fine healer, and the people trust you. The village will thrive under your care."

"But why now?" Mira asked, her voice breaking. "Why do you have to leave?"

Elora hesitated, choosing her words carefully. "Because... there are things happening in the world, things that are dangerous. I've felt it for some time now—an imbalance in the earth's magic. Something dark is stirring, and I can't stay here if it reaches us."

Mira's eyes filled with fear. "Dark magic?"

Elora nodded. "Yes. The old ones—ancient beings who once tried to take the magic of the earth for themselves. They were banished long ago, but now I fear they're stirring again. I can't explain it fully, but I can feel their presence growing stronger."

Mira swallowed hard, her face pale. "What do we do?"

Elora squeezed her shoulder gently. "You stay here, and you protect the village. I've trained you well, Mira. You're stronger than you think. As for me... I have to go. There are things I need to face."

Mira opened her mouth to protest, but before she could speak, there was a knock at the door. Elora's heart skipped a beat, her senses immediately on alert. She hadn't been expecting anyone, and the energy outside the door felt... strange. Unfamiliar.

She moved to the door and opened it slowly, her breath catching in her throat when she saw who stood on the other side.

A man, tall and cloaked in shadows, his face hidden beneath a hood. But his presence was unmistakable. Elora hadn't seen him in centuries, but she would never forget the feel of his magic—the way it hummed with an intensity that bordered on danger.

"Aidan," she said, her voice tight with both surprise and apprehension.

The man lowered his hood, revealing a face that had not aged a day since the last time she had seen him. His dark hair was swept back, and his eyes—sharp, piercing—met hers with a flicker of something unreadable.

"Elora," he said, his voice low and familiar. "It's been a long time."

Elora felt her heart clench. She had known Aidan centuries ago, during a time of great upheaval. They had been allies once, though she had never fully trusted him. His motives had always been shrouded in mystery, and now, after all these years, he had found her again.

"What are you doing here?" Elora asked, her voice tense.

Aidan stepped forward, his expression serious. "I've come to warn you. The darkness you've felt—it's already here. And it's coming for you."

Elora's blood ran cold.

Chapter 2: Echoes of the Past

The world seemed to hold its breath as Elora stared at Aidan, her heart hammering in her chest. The air in the room thickened with tension, the weight of the past pressing down on her. Aidan's words echoed in her mind, the warning sharp and clear: *It's coming for you.*

Mira shifted behind her, her presence a quiet, nervous energy that Elora could feel without turning to look. Elora closed the door softly, stepping out into the crisp evening air. The sky above them had darkened, the twilight bleeding into the inky night, a reminder that time was slipping away from them.

Aidan watched her, his expression unreadable, but Elora knew him too well. Beneath his calm demeanor, there was something more—urgency, perhaps even fear. And that alone was enough to send a chill through her. Aidan had never been one to show fear, not in all the centuries they had known each other.

"Why now?" Elora asked, her voice low and steady, though the unease coiled tightly in her chest. "Why are they coming for me now?"

Aidan glanced around, as if ensuring they were alone, before stepping closer. His voice was a quiet murmur, meant only for her ears. "The old ones are no longer just stirring, Elora. They've found a way to reach into the world again, and they've been searching for you. They always have been. But something's changed. They know where you are now. They know what you hold inside you."

Elora felt the blood drain from her face. She had always known the old ones would never truly stop hunting for the power of the old gods. That was why she had lived in the shadows, why she had moved from place to place for centuries, never staying long enough for anyone to learn her secret. But Aidan's words struck a deeper fear within her. They knew. And that meant she could no longer hide.

"How do they know?" Elora asked, though she feared the answer.

"They've been using conduits," Aidan replied, his tone grave. "Mortals imbued with fragments of their magic. Through them, they've been able to drain the earth's magic, slowly weakening the seals that keep them bound. And through them, they've sensed you. They know you're the last of the old gods. The power you carry—it's the key to breaking the final seal."

Elora's breath caught in her throat. *The final seal.* The very thought of it sent a wave of nausea through her. If the old ones broke free, the world would unravel. The magic of the earth, already fragile and frayed, would be torn apart, consumed by their hunger for power. Everything she had protected, everything she had sacrificed, would be lost.

She turned away, her gaze drifting to the darkened forest beyond the village. The trees swayed gently in the evening breeze, their whispers soft but urgent, as if they, too, felt the threat that loomed just beyond the horizon.

"I can't stay here," Elora said, her voice thick with the weight of the decision. "If they're coming for me, I can't put the village at risk."

Aidan stepped closer, his voice firm but gentle. "You were never meant to stay in one place forever. You know that as well as I do. But this time, it's different. You can't run from them, Elora. Not anymore."

Elora felt the words like a blow. She had spent centuries running, always staying ahead of the danger, always slipping away before anyone could get too close. But Aidan was right. This time, there was no more running.

She turned to face him, her eyes searching his. "What do you expect me to do, Aidan? Fight them?"

His gaze didn't waver. "Yes."

Elora laughed bitterly, though there was no humor in the sound. "You know what that would mean. If I fight them, if I use my power—"

"They'll know exactly where you are," Aidan finished, his voice quiet. "But that's why you have to face them. You can't hide from this anymore."

Elora's chest tightened, her heart pounding against her ribs. She had avoided using her full power for centuries, keeping it locked away, using only what was necessary to heal, to protect. She had feared what it would mean to unleash it, feared the attention it would draw. But now, it seemed, there was no other choice.

"And what happens when they take it?" she asked, her voice shaking despite herself. "What happens when they break the seal and they take the power of the old gods?"

Aidan's jaw clenched. "That's why I'm here. We won't let them take it."

Elora let out a shaky breath, her mind racing. She had spent so long avoiding this—avoiding the very thing she had been created to do. But now, as the darkness closed in, she knew that the time for hiding was over.

Mira appeared in the doorway, her eyes wide with concern. "Elora? What's happening?"

Elora turned to her, her heart breaking a little at the sight of her young apprentice. Mira had so much to learn, so much life ahead of her. But now, Elora would have to leave her behind.

"I have to go, Mira," Elora said softly, stepping forward to place a hand on her shoulder. "There are things happening in the world—things I need to stop."

Mira shook her head, tears welling in her eyes. "But you can't! The village needs you! I need you!"

Elora's chest tightened, the weight of her responsibilities crashing down on her. She knelt in front of Mira, taking both of her hands in hers. "You're strong, Mira. Stronger than you know. You've learned everything I can teach you. The village will need you now, and I know you'll protect them."

Mira's lip quivered, her voice breaking. "But where will you go? When will you come back?"

Elora forced a smile, though her heart ached with the knowledge that she might not return. "I'll find you again. When it's safe, I'll come back."

THE ETERNAL CIRCLE

Mira flung her arms around Elora, holding her tightly. Elora closed her eyes, willing herself to hold back the tears that threatened to fall. She had done this before—left behind people she cared for, knowing she might never see them again. But this time felt different. This time, the danger was greater, the stakes higher.

When Mira finally pulled back, Elora rose to her feet, turning to Aidan. "Where do we go?"

Aidan's eyes flickered with relief, though his face remained stoic. "There's a place, far to the north. A sanctuary. We'll regroup there, gather allies. But we'll need to move quickly. The old ones won't wait."

Elora nodded, feeling the weight of her decision settle over her like a heavy cloak. She turned back to Mira one last time. "Stay safe. Protect the village."

Mira wiped at her eyes, nodding as she stepped back into the doorway. "I will."

Without another word, Elora and Aidan stepped into the shadows, the cold wind biting at their skin as they left the village behind. The path ahead was uncertain, the danger far greater than anything Elora had faced before. But now, there was no turning back.

The night deepened as they traveled through the dense forest, the only sounds the crunch of leaves beneath their feet and the distant calls of nocturnal creatures. The darkness wrapped around them, but Elora could feel the old ones out there, somewhere in the distance. Their presence was a dark stain on the magic of the earth, a force that pulsed with hunger and greed.

"How long do we have?" Elora asked quietly, her voice barely breaking the silence.

Aidan's face was grim. "Not long. Days, maybe less."

Elora swallowed hard. She had always known the old ones would come for her eventually. But now that the moment was here, the fear gnawed at her insides like a relentless ache.

"They've been waiting for centuries," Aidan continued. "But now that they've sensed you, they won't stop until they've taken what you carry."

Elora's hands clenched into fists. The power of the old gods, the magic she had been given to protect the earth, was a beacon to the old ones. They had always wanted it, always hungered for the power that had been denied to them. And now, they were closer than ever.

"We can stop them," Aidan said, his voice filled with quiet determination. "We've done it before. We'll do it again."

Elora nodded, though her heart still raced with fear. She had fought the old ones before, centuries ago, when they had first tried to take the magic of the earth. But the battles had been brutal, and the cost had been high. She had barely survived the last time. And now, she was alone. The other gods were gone, their power lost to the ages. Only she remained.

And if she fell, the world would fall with her.

"We'll need to gather others," Aidan said, breaking through her thoughts. "There are still those out there who remember the old ways. They'll fight with us."

Elora nodded, though doubt tugged at the edges of her mind. Could they really stop the old ones? Could they really protect the magic of the earth from beings as ancient and powerful as the old gods themselves?

As they continued through the darkened forest, the trees whispered warnings in a language only Elora could understand. The earth beneath her feet trembled with fear, the magic of the land fraying at the edges. The old ones were coming, and soon, the final battle would begin.

For now, all Elora could do was move forward, one step at a time, into the darkness that lay ahead.

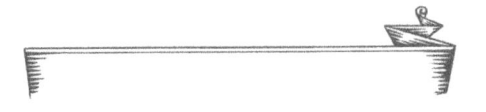

Chapter 3: The Gathering Shadows

The deeper Elora and Aidan ventured into the forest, the more the world seemed to change around them. The trees grew taller and darker, their branches twisting like skeletal fingers reaching toward the sky. The air thickened, charged with the unmistakable hum of magic. Elora could feel it—dark tendrils of power snaking through the earth, seeking something, someone. They were closer than she had realized.

Aidan led the way, his movements sure but tense. He had always been confident, always capable, but even now, she could see the weight of the situation pressing down on him. The old ones were not just ancient enemies—they were a threat far greater than any mortal or magical being could imagine. And they were hunting her.

"Are you sure this sanctuary is safe?" Elora asked, her voice barely more than a whisper as they pushed deeper into the forest.

Aidan glanced over his shoulder, his expression unreadable in the dim light. "Safe enough. For now."

Elora raised an eyebrow, though she wasn't surprised by his vague response. Aidan had always been one for secrets, even in the days when they had fought side by side. But something about this situation felt different. The old ones had found her, and there would be no hiding from them this time.

"What is this place, exactly?" she pressed, sensing that there was more to the sanctuary than he had let on.

Aidan hesitated, his gaze sweeping the shadows around them before he answered. "It's a place where the magic of the earth is still strong. A nexus of power, untouched by the old ones. There are others like you, beings who have been hiding for centuries. They've gathered there, waiting for the right moment to strike back."

Elora's heart tightened at his words. Others like her? She had spent so long believing she was the last—isolated, alone with her burden of immortality and power. The idea that there were others, that they had been hiding just as she had, both intrigued and unsettled her.

"How many?" she asked, her voice soft but steady.

"Not many," Aidan replied. "But enough. Enough to fight."

Elora's mind raced as she considered the implications. If there were others like her—ancient beings tied to the old magic—then perhaps there was a chance to stop the old ones. But it wouldn't be easy. The power the old ones sought was unlike anything mortal magic could comprehend. It was raw, pure, and limitless. And it was locked inside her.

They walked in silence for what felt like hours, the forest growing darker and more oppressive with every step. Elora's senses were on high alert, the earth beneath her feet vibrating with the presence of something dark and dangerous. The old ones were close, she could feel them. Their magic pulsed in the distance, a low, steady thrum that reverberated through the earth like a warning.

THE ETERNAL CIRCLE 25

Finally, after what felt like an eternity, they reached a clearing. In the center stood a cluster of ancient stone structures, worn down by time but still humming with power. The air here was different—thicker, charged with magic that made Elora's skin tingle. She could feel the pulse of the earth, strong and steady, as though this place was a living, breathing entity.

"The sanctuary," Aidan said quietly, his voice filled with a reverence she hadn't heard from him before.

Elora stepped forward, her eyes scanning the structures. They were old, older than any mortal civilization she had encountered in her lifetimes. The stones were covered in intricate carvings, runes that glowed faintly in the twilight. This place wasn't just a refuge—it was sacred, a place where the magic of the earth had been nurtured and protected for centuries.

As they approached, figures began to emerge from the shadows. Elora's heart quickened as she took in the sight of them—beings like her, ageless and powerful, each one radiating a different kind of magic. Some were tall and regal, their features sharp and ethereal, while others appeared more human, though there was no mistaking the ancient power that thrummed beneath their skin.

One of them stepped forward, a woman with silver hair that shimmered like moonlight. Her eyes were piercing, her presence commanding, and Elora could feel the weight of centuries in her gaze.

"You must be Elora," the woman said, her voice soft but filled with authority.

Elora nodded, her eyes meeting the woman's. "And you are?"

"**Lirael**," the woman replied, inclining her head slightly in greeting. "I've heard much about you."

Elora didn't miss the flicker of curiosity in Lirael's eyes, nor the subtle tension in the air around them. It was clear that her arrival had been anticipated, but not necessarily welcomed.

"Then you know why I'm here," Elora said, her voice steady despite the unease building in her chest.

Lirael nodded. "The old ones have begun to stir. We've felt their presence, seen the effects of their dark magic on the land. But we didn't realize they had found you."

"They have," Aidan interjected, his voice grim. "And they're coming for her."

A ripple of unease passed through the group, the weight of Aidan's words settling over them like a heavy fog. The other beings exchanged glances, their expressions darkening as the reality of the situation sank in.

"They've been waiting for this moment for centuries," Lirael said, her gaze returning to Elora. "The power you hold... it's what they've always wanted. And now that they've found you, they won't stop until they've taken it."

Elora felt a cold knot form in her stomach. She had known this moment would come, had felt it looming on the horizon for as long as she could remember. But now, standing here, surrounded by beings who were supposed to be her allies, the weight of her burden felt heavier than ever.

"What do you expect me to do?" Elora asked, her voice tight.

Lirael's expression softened slightly, though there was still an edge of tension in her gaze. "We expect you to help us stop them. Your power... it's the only thing that can keep the old ones from breaking free."

Elora clenched her fists, the weight of her responsibility pressing down on her like a suffocating blanket. She had spent centuries avoiding this—avoiding the very thing she had been created for. But now, it seemed, there was no escaping it.

"And if they take it?" Elora asked, her voice barely above a whisper.

Lirael's eyes darkened. "Then the world as we know it will end."

The silence that followed was thick with tension. Elora could feel the eyes of everyone in the clearing on her, waiting for her response, waiting for her to step into the role they believed she was meant to play. But all Elora could feel was the overwhelming fear that had been gnawing at her for centuries.

She turned away, her gaze drifting to the darkened forest beyond the sanctuary. The old ones were out there, somewhere, their presence a constant, dark pulse in the back of her mind. They were closer than ever, and soon, they would come for her.

Elora took a deep breath, steadying herself. She had spent too long running, too long hiding from her destiny. Now, the time for hiding was over.

"I'll fight," Elora said finally, her voice steady despite the fear swirling inside her. "But I won't do it alone."

Aidan stepped forward, his expression filled with quiet determination. "You won't have to."

Lirael nodded, though her gaze remained cautious. "We'll stand with you, Elora. But you must understand—the old ones won't stop until they've taken everything. This fight won't be easy."

Elora met her gaze, her heart heavy but resolute. "It never is."

That night, Elora sat alone at the edge of the sanctuary, the cool wind brushing against her skin as she stared out into the darkness. The others had dispersed, each preparing in their own way for the battle that lay ahead. But Elora couldn't shake the feeling that something was wrong—something deeper than the threat of the old ones.

The power inside her, the power of the old gods, had always been a part of her. It had been both her gift and her burden, a constant reminder of the responsibility she carried. But now, as the danger grew closer, she wondered if she could control it. If she could truly wield the power that had been entrusted to her without losing herself in the process.

Sorin padded over to her, his golden eyes gleaming in the darkness. He pressed his head against her leg, his presence comforting in the silence.

"I don't know if I can do this," Elora whispered, her voice barely audible over the wind. "What if I lose control?"

Sorin didn't respond, but Elora felt the warmth of his loyalty and his silent support. He had been with her through lifetimes, through moments of triumph and despair, and though he couldn't speak, Elora knew he understood her fears better than anyone.

She reached down, running her fingers through his thick fur, grounding herself in his presence. The old ones were coming. The fight was inevitable. But for now, in this quiet moment, Elora allowed herself to simply breathe.

For now, that was enough.

But when the storm arrived, she would be ready. She had to be.

Chapter 4: The Weight of Immortality

The morning came heavy and cold, the once soft hum of the sanctuary now charged with tension. The pulse of magic was tangible, threading through the air, wrapping around the stones, and filling every crevice. The sky above was a muted gray, the promise of a storm looming in the distance. Elora stood at the edge of the sanctuary, her eyes tracing the distant horizon where dark clouds gathered, thick and ominous. She could feel the earth trembling beneath her feet, a subtle vibration that told her the old ones were drawing closer. The sanctuary, once a place of refuge, now felt fragile, as though it could shatter under the weight of what was to come.

Her mind was still reeling from the previous night's conversation with Lirael and the others. She had agreed to fight, agreed to confront the old ones, but deep down, fear gnawed at her. It wasn't fear of the old ones themselves, but of what she might become in the process. The power of the old gods was still buried deep within her, an untapped well of magic that she had kept locked away for centuries. What would happen when she unleashed it?

The world had always seen her as a healer, a guardian of the earth's magic. But her powers were far greater than healing. The truth was something she had hidden from even those closest to her. She had the ability to tear the earth apart, to bend nature to her will, to bring life—and death. She had chosen to keep that part of herself hidden, fearing what she might do if she let the full force of her power surface.

Sorin padded up beside her, his silent presence a comfort. He nuzzled her leg gently, sensing her unease. Elora glanced down at him, a small smile tugging at the corners of her lips. She knelt beside him, running her hand through his fur. "What would I do without you?" she whispered, her voice barely carrying over the wind.

Sorin's golden eyes held hers for a moment, steady and calm, as if telling her that no matter what happened, he would stand by her. Elora leaned her forehead against his, drawing strength from his quiet loyalty.

Footsteps behind her broke the silence. She didn't need to turn to know it was Aidan. His presence had a weight to it, a mix of old memories and unspoken truths that had lingered between them for centuries.

"We need to talk," Aidan said, his voice low but firm.

Elora straightened, standing as she turned to face him. His eyes were dark with worry, but beneath the worry, there was something else—determination, perhaps even desperation.

"About what?" Elora asked, though she had a feeling she already knew.

Aidan crossed his arms, glancing at the sky before meeting her gaze again. "You're still holding back. Last night, when you agreed to fight, you didn't fully commit. I can see it in your eyes."

Elora bristled, her defenses rising instinctively. "You think I'm not taking this seriously?"

"I think you're afraid," Aidan said bluntly, his words cutting through the air like a blade.

Elora stiffened, her chest tightening. "Of course I'm afraid. The old ones are coming, Aidan. They want to tear this world apart, and if they get to me, to the power I carry—"

"They won't," Aidan interrupted, stepping closer. "Because we won't let them. But you need to stop running from what you are."

Elora's breath caught in her throat. She had spent centuries avoiding this, hiding from the full truth of her existence. But Aidan had always known. He had seen her power once, long ago, in a battle they had fought side by side. He knew what she was capable of, even if she had spent lifetimes trying to forget.

"I can't," she whispered, her voice barely audible over the wind. "If I let that part of me loose—if I lose control—"

"You won't lose control," Aidan said, his voice firm but gentle. "You've spent centuries learning, mastering every aspect of your power. You're not a child who can't control her magic anymore. You're stronger than you think."

Elora looked away, her eyes tracing the edges of the distant mountains. She wanted to believe him, but the fear still gripped her heart like a vice. She had seen what unchecked power could do. She had witnessed entire cities crumble beneath the wrath of beings who thought they were untouchable. She didn't want to become one of them.

Aidan stepped closer, his voice softening. "Elora, the old ones are closer than ever. They're draining the magic from the earth, and soon they'll come for you. We need your strength, your power. You were given the gift of the old gods for a reason."

Elora's chest tightened. The responsibility weighed on her like a mountain. She had spent so long moving from place to place, keeping her distance from the world, teaching only what was necessary. But now, with the threat looming over them, she knew she couldn't hide any longer.

"I'm not sure I can do it," Elora admitted, her voice thick with emotion. "I've spent centuries running from this."

Aidan reached out, placing a hand on her arm. His touch was warm, steady. "You're not alone anymore. We're in this together. We'll fight together."

Elora looked up at him, searching his eyes. For a moment, she saw a flicker of something deeper—an emotion she hadn't allowed herself to acknowledge in centuries. It was a reminder of the connection they had shared long ago, before everything had changed.

She took a deep breath, trying to steady herself. "I'll fight. But I need you to understand—I won't be able to hold back."

Aidan nodded, his eyes holding hers with quiet intensity. "I wouldn't expect you to."

The day passed in a blur of preparations. Lirael and Dorin gathered the others, organizing supplies, setting protective wards around the sanctuary, and preparing for what was to come. Elora could feel the magic in the air growing denser, more charged, as if the earth itself was bracing for the coming storm.

As the sun began to dip below the horizon, casting the sky in hues of deep purple and gold, the sanctuary became a hive of activity. The other beings who had gathered here—guardians of the old ways, ancient beings like herself—moved with purpose. Some sharpened weapons imbued with old magic, while others whispered incantations, their voices blending with the hum of the earth's magic.

Elora stood apart from them, her eyes scanning the horizon. She could feel it—the darkness creeping closer, the weight of the old ones' magic pressing against the boundaries of the world. They were drawing nearer, and with each passing moment, the pull of the power inside her grew stronger.

"They'll be here soon," Lirael said quietly, stepping up beside her. Her silver hair shimmered in the fading light, her face calm but resolute.

Elora nodded, her heart pounding in her chest. "I know."

Lirael's gaze shifted to her, studying her for a long moment. "I've heard stories about you, Elora. About the power you carry. Some say you're the last of the old gods, that you've lived for so long because you're tied to the very essence of the earth."

Elora's jaw tightened. "I'm not a god."

Lirael raised an eyebrow. "Aren't you?"

Elora looked away, her mind swirling with the weight of her past. She had been given the power of the old gods, yes, but she had never considered herself one of them. She had always been more of a guardian, a protector of the earth, not a deity to be worshiped.

"I was given a gift," Elora said finally. "A gift I never asked for. And now, it's a burden."

Lirael's gaze softened, her voice gentle. "A burden, perhaps. But also a responsibility. You were chosen for a reason, Elora. And that reason is becoming clear now."

Elora's chest tightened. She had spent so long avoiding this moment, trying to live quietly, to avoid the inevitable. But now, as the darkness drew closer, she knew she couldn't run any longer.

"What if I fail?" Elora whispered, her voice barely audible over the wind.

Lirael placed a hand on her shoulder, her touch warm and reassuring. "You won't."

Elora met her gaze, seeing the quiet confidence in her eyes. It was a confidence Elora wasn't sure she shared, but it was enough to steady her, if only for the moment.

"We're ready for them," Lirael said, her voice filled with resolve. "But we need your strength."

Elora nodded, though the fear still coiled tightly in her chest. She had agreed to fight, to face the old ones, but the thought of unleashing the full extent of her power terrified her. She had spent centuries holding it back, keeping it locked away. What would happen when she let it loose?

As the last of the sunlight disappeared and the night descended, the air around them grew thick with anticipation. The old ones were coming. Elora could feel their presence in the distance, like a dark storm on the horizon, their magic seeping through the earth like poison.

The sanctuary was no longer a place of peace. It had become a battlefield waiting for the first strike.

And when that strike came, Elora knew there would be no turning back.

The night was still, unnaturally quiet, as if the world itself was holding its breath. Elora stood at the center of the sanctuary, surrounded by the ancient stones and the guardians

THE ETERNAL CIRCLE

who had gathered here to fight. The magic in the air crackled, a raw, untamed force that set her skin tingling.

Aidan was beside her, his sword drawn, his eyes scanning the darkness beyond the sanctuary. Lirael and Dorin stood on either side, their magic weaving around them like protective shields.

The old ones were close. Elora could feel them pressing against the edge of the world, trying to break through. Their dark magic pulsed through the earth, a slow, relentless force that made her heart pound in her chest.

Suddenly, the air shifted. A ripple of magic spread through the sanctuary, a cold, bone-chilling wave that sent a shudder down Elora's spine.

"They're here," Aidan said, his voice low and steady.

Elora's breath hitched as she felt the first flicker of the old ones' presence—dark, ancient, and filled with hunger. They had come for her. They had come for the power she carried, the power they had coveted for centuries.

Her heart raced, the fear swirling inside her like a storm. But there was no more time for fear.

It was time to fight.

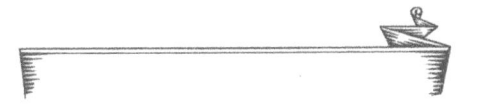

Chapter 5: The Awakening of Power

The air itself seemed to hold its breath as the shadows thickened around the sanctuary. Elora stood at the center, her heart pounding in time with the pulse of the earth beneath her feet. The old ones were closer than ever. She could feel their dark presence pressing against the boundaries of the world, seeking a way in. The night was still, the silence so profound it felt as though the entire world had paused, waiting for the first blow to fall.

Beside her, Aidan's grip tightened on the hilt of his sword, the tension radiating from him palpable. The others—Lirael, Dorin, and the small group of ancient beings who had gathered here to fight—stood in a wide circle around the sacred stones. Each one of them was poised, their magic crackling in the air like static, ready to defend the sanctuary from whatever came through the darkness.

But Elora knew the truth. The old ones weren't coming for them. They were coming for her.

She had been running from this moment for centuries, always moving from place to place, never staying long enough for anyone to notice how she never aged, how she carried a power far greater than any mortal could understand. But the time for running was over. The old ones had found her. And now, they wanted what was inside her—the power of the old gods.

Elora's breath came in shallow gasps as she reached deep within herself, feeling the ancient magic stir in response to the threat. It was still there, buried deep, waiting. She had kept it locked away for so long, refusing to tap into the full extent of her power for fear of what it might do to her, to the world around her. But now, as the darkness pressed in, she knew she had no choice.

Her fingers curled into fists as the earth trembled beneath her feet, the first ripple of the old ones' magic slipping through the barrier. It was cold, dark, and full of malice, like the breath of a storm just before it breaks.

"They're coming," Aidan said quietly, his voice tight with tension.

Elora nodded, her pulse quickening. "I can feel them."

The others shifted, their gazes fixed on the darkness beyond the sanctuary, where the shadows seemed to writhe and twist like living things. The air was heavy with anticipation, thick with magic that buzzed in Elora's ears. She could feel the old ones reaching, clawing at the fabric of the world, trying to tear it open.

Suddenly, the air exploded with a deafening crack, and the ground beneath their feet shuddered violently. The barrier that had protected the sanctuary buckled under the pressure, and for a brief moment, Elora felt the world split open. A cold, black wind swept through the clearing, and with it came the presence of the old ones—ancient, malevolent, and hungry.

Dark figures emerged from the shadows, their forms barely discernible, like smoke given life. Their eyes glowed with an unnatural light, and their movements were slow, deliberate, as if they were savoring the fear that hung in the air.

"They've broken through," Lirael whispered, her voice laced with dread.

Elora's heart raced as she felt the pull of the old ones' magic, a dark tendril of power reaching toward her, seeking the magic she carried. Her chest tightened, and for a moment, she couldn't breathe. She had always known they would come for her, but the reality of it was far more terrifying than she had imagined.

"Get ready," Aidan said, his voice steady despite the chaos that swirled around them.

The others braced themselves, their magic flaring to life in a brilliant display of light and power. Lirael's silver hair glowed with an ethereal light as she summoned her magic, while Dorin's fists crackled with energy, ready to strike. But Elora knew it wouldn't be enough. The old ones weren't like anything they had faced before. They were ancient beings of pure magic, and the only thing that could stop them was the power she carried—the power of the old gods.

Elora took a deep breath, her heart pounding in her ears as she reached deep within herself, feeling the magic stir, sluggish at first, then with growing intensity. The earth beneath her feet responded, the pulse of life and magic intertwining with her own, filling her with strength. The power of the old gods thrummed in her veins, a force so immense it made her head spin.

She had kept this part of herself hidden for so long, afraid of what it might do if she let it loose. But now, as the darkness closed in, she knew she couldn't hold back any longer.

"Elora," Aidan said, his voice tight with urgency. "We need you."

Elora's gaze snapped to the dark figures advancing through the clearing. Their eyes glowed with hunger, their dark forms flickering like shadows in the wind. The magic they carried was cold and deadly, a force that sought to consume everything in its path.

Her hands trembled as she raised them, her magic surging in response to the threat. The earth beneath her feet pulsed, and the air around her vibrated with power. She could feel the old gods' magic rising inside her, filling her with strength, with purpose.

This was what she had been created for.

The old ones let out a low, guttural hiss, their dark energy spreading like a shadow across the ground, reaching toward the stones of the sanctuary. The others moved to intercept, their magic flaring to life as they prepared to fight. But Elora knew this battle wasn't theirs. It was hers.

She took a deep breath, closing her eyes as she let the power of the earth flow through her, filling her with the strength of the old gods. The magic surged, wild and untamed, threatening to overwhelm her, but she held on, forcing herself to stay in control.

When she opened her eyes, the world around her seemed to slow. The dark figures of the old ones moved with a strange, deliberate grace, their magic reaching out like tendrils, seeking to pull her in. But Elora was ready.

With a single, sharp movement, she unleashed the power inside her.

THE ETERNAL CIRCLE 43

The earth beneath her feet erupted, sending a wave of raw, untamed magic crashing toward the old ones. The ground split open, and the air crackled with energy as the power of the old gods surged through the clearing. The force of it was immense, a tidal wave of magic that tore through the darkness, scattering the old ones like leaves in the wind.

For a moment, the clearing was filled with light—pure, brilliant light that burned away the shadows and drove the darkness back. The old ones hissed and recoiled, their forms flickering as they were forced to retreat, their dark magic no match for the power that Elora wielded.

But it wasn't over.

As the last of the light faded, the old ones regrouped, their dark forms coalescing into something more solid, more dangerous. Their eyes burned with a new intensity, and their magic crackled in the air, dark and twisted.

"They're not done yet," Aidan muttered, his grip tightening on his sword.

Elora's heart pounded in her chest as she felt the magic inside her surge again, stronger this time, more insistent. The power of the old gods was rising, pushing her to unleash it fully, to let it flow freely through her. But she hesitated. She knew that once she let it loose, there would be no going back.

"Elora!" Aidan's voice snapped her out of her thoughts, and she turned to see the old ones advancing again, their dark magic spreading like a stain across the ground.

Her hands shook as she raised them again, the magic inside her roaring to life. The earth responded, the stones around her glowing with ancient runes as the power of the old gods flowed through her. The air crackled with energy, and the sky above them darkened, as if the world itself was bracing for what was to come.

With a single thought, Elora unleashed the full force of her power.

The ground beneath her feet split open, and a torrent of magic surged through the clearing, a blinding wave of light and energy that tore through the old ones' defenses. The dark figures let out a deafening wail as they were engulfed by the magic, their forms dissolving into nothingness as the power of the old gods consumed them.

The earth trembled, and the air filled with the crackle of energy as the last of the old ones were driven back, their dark magic shattered by the force of Elora's power. The ground shook violently, and for a moment, the world seemed to hang in the balance.

Then, as quickly as it had begun, the magic dissipated, leaving the clearing in a deafening silence.

Elora stood in the center of it all, her body trembling from the exertion, her heart pounding in her chest. The power inside her had quieted, but it still thrummed beneath the surface, waiting, watching.

The old ones were gone. The sanctuary was safe. But Elora knew this wasn't the end.

This was only the beginning.

Chapter 6: After the Storm

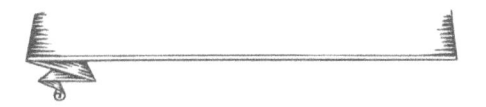

The silence that followed the battle was suffocating, an eerie calm settling over the sanctuary as if the world itself was holding its breath. The earth beneath Elora's feet still trembled faintly, the last echoes of her magic reverberating through the ground. The old ones were gone—at least for now—but the aftermath of the power she had unleashed left her shaken.

The others stood in stunned silence, their eyes wide with awe and fear as they took in the aftermath. The air still crackled with the remnants of her magic, a raw, untamed force that had driven back the darkness but had left a mark on the sanctuary. The stones that had once glowed with ancient runes were now scorched, the ground blackened and cracked where her power had torn through it.

Elora's breath came in ragged gasps as she slowly lowered her hands, the magic inside her quieting, though it still pulsed beneath the surface. Her limbs felt heavy, her muscles weak, as if the power had drained every ounce of strength from her body. She could feel the weight of her actions pressing down on her, the burden of what she had done.

She had unleashed the full force of her power—something she had sworn never to do. The old gods' magic had coursed through her like a river of fire, a force so immense it had nearly consumed her. And yet, even now, as the danger seemed to have passed, she felt a deep unease settling in her chest.

Had she gone too far?

Aidan was the first to break the silence. He stepped forward, his expression unreadable, though his eyes flickered with something she couldn't quite place—concern, perhaps, or something deeper.

"Elora," he said softly, his voice cutting through the stillness. "Are you all right?"

Elora nodded, though she wasn't entirely sure she was telling the truth. Her body felt hollow, her mind clouded with the weight of what had just transpired. The old ones had been driven back, but the power she had tapped into—the sheer force of it—left her unsettled.

"I'm fine," she said, though her voice lacked conviction.

Aidan's gaze remained steady, but he didn't press her. Instead, he glanced around at the others, who were still standing in shock, their faces pale. Lirael, usually so composed, looked shaken, her silver hair disheveled, her eyes wide as she stared at the scorched earth where the battle had taken place.

"You did it," Lirael whispered, her voice filled with awe and disbelief. "You stopped them."

Elora forced herself to take a deep breath, trying to shake off the lingering sensation of the old gods' power still humming through her veins. "For now," she said quietly. "But they'll be back. And next time, they'll be stronger."

Lirael's face tightened with concern. "What do you mean?"

Elora glanced at the darkened horizon, where the faint traces of the old ones' magic still lingered like a shadow.

"They've tasted my power now. They'll find another way. This was only the beginning."

A heavy silence fell over the group as the reality of her words sank in. The old ones weren't gone—they had been forced back, but they would return. And when they did, they would be even more determined to take what Elora carried.

Aidan stepped closer, his eyes searching hers. "We'll be ready," he said, his voice filled with quiet determination.

Elora nodded, though she wasn't sure she shared his confidence. She had fought them off this time, but at what cost? The power she had unleashed had left a mark on the earth, a scar that couldn't be erased. The sanctuary, once a place of peace and refuge, now felt fractured, as if the very fabric of the world had been torn open.

"We need to regroup," Dorin said, his voice low but steady. "They'll come again, and we can't afford to be caught off guard."

Lirael nodded in agreement. "There are others like us—scattered, hidden. We need to find them, bring them together. We can't fight this alone."

Elora's heart sank at the thought of more battles, more destruction. The world was already fragile, its magic fraying at the edges, and every clash with the old ones only weakened it further. But she knew they were right. They couldn't fight this alone.

"We'll need to find the remaining sanctuaries," Aidan said, his eyes narrowing in thought. "There are places where the old magic is still strong. We can fortify them, make a stand."

Elora's gaze drifted to the horizon, where the last traces of the battle lingered like a distant memory. The idea of fortifying sanctuaries, of gathering their allies, felt like grasping at straws. But it was all they had.

"I'll go with you," Elora said softly, though her voice wavered. "We'll find the others. But we need to be careful. The old ones are getting stronger, and if they find us again..."

Aidan nodded, understanding the weight of her words. "We'll stay ahead of them."

Elora wanted to believe him, but deep down, the fear still gnawed at her. She had tasted the full extent of her power, and while it had saved them this time, it had also left her vulnerable. The more she used it, the more the old ones would be drawn to her, their hunger for the power of the old gods growing stronger with each encounter.

"We leave at first light," Lirael said, her voice steady once more as she took command of the situation. "We'll need supplies, and we should reinforce the wards around the sanctuary in case they come back."

The others nodded, though the tension in the air was thick. They had won this battle, but it felt like a fleeting victory—a temporary reprieve in the face of a much larger storm.

As the others dispersed, each heading off to prepare for the journey ahead, Elora remained where she was, her eyes fixed on the scorched earth where her magic had torn through the darkness. The ground was cracked and blackened; the ancient runes that had once protected the sanctuary now marred by the force of her power.

She knelt down, running her fingers over the scorched earth. The magic of the old gods still lingered here, a reminder of what she had unleashed. She had always been careful, always restrained, but now she had seen what happened when she let

THE ETERNAL CIRCLE

go. The power had been overwhelming—both exhilarating and terrifying. And it had left her shaken.

Sorin appeared at her side, his large, comforting presence grounding her. He pressed his head against her arm, as if sensing her turmoil. Elora closed her eyes, drawing comfort from his warmth, from the steady presence that had been with her for so long.

"I don't know if I can do this," she whispered, her voice trembling with the weight of her doubt.

Sorin didn't respond, but his quiet loyalty was enough. He had seen her through lifetimes, through moments of despair and triumph, and now, as the world seemed to teeter on the edge of darkness, he was still with her.

Elora took a deep breath, standing slowly as she gathered her thoughts. The battle wasn't over. The old ones were still out there, and they would come again. But she couldn't let fear stop her. She had a responsibility—to the earth, to the magic she had been entrusted with, and to the people who had placed their faith in her.

As she looked out at the darkened horizon, the weight of her immortality settled over her once more. She had lived for centuries, seen civilizations rise and fall, and now, in this fragile moment, she stood at the center of it all.

The old ones would return. And when they did, Elora would be ready.

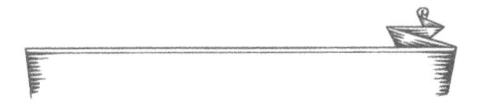

Chapter 7: The Road to the Sanctuaries

At dawn, the sanctuary was bathed in the soft light of the rising sun, casting long shadows across the stones and trees. The air was crisp and still, a fragile peace settling over the clearing after the chaos of the night before. But beneath the surface, tension simmered, the unspoken fear of what lay ahead weighing on everyone's shoulders.

Elora stood at the edge of the clearing, watching as the others prepared for their journey. Lirael and Dorin were speaking in hushed tones, their faces tight with concentration as they discussed the best route to take. Aidan was off to the side, checking his weapons, his expression grim.

Elora's body still ached from the magic she had unleashed, a dull, lingering pain that reminded her of the power she had wielded. Her hands trembled slightly as she tightened the strap on her pack, trying to shake off the fatigue that clung to her.

"We're ready," Aidan said as he approached, his voice low but steady.

Elora nodded, though the knot of anxiety in her chest hadn't lessened. "Where are we going first?"

"There's a sanctuary to the north," Lirael replied, stepping forward. "Hidden deep in the mountains. It's one of the last places where the old magic still holds strong."

"Will the others meet us there?" Dorin asked, his brow furrowed.

Lirael glanced at Elora before answering. "If they're still alive."

Elora's heart sank at the thought. The other sanctuaries, the places of refuge where magic had been kept safe for centuries, were vulnerable now. The old ones would be seeking them out, draining the magic, tearing them apart. There was no guarantee that anyone would be waiting for them when they arrived.

"We'll find them," Aidan said, his voice filled with quiet determination. "We'll gather our allies, and we'll stop the old ones before they can destroy anything else."

Elora wanted to believe him, but the doubt still gnawed at her. The battle ahead felt impossibly large, and the cost of failure was too great to contemplate.

As the group gathered at the edge of the sanctuary, preparing to set off on their journey, Elora took one last look at the scorched earth behind her. This had been a place of peace and healing for so long. But now, it was a battleground, and the world outside was full of dangers she could no longer ignore.

"We'll come back," Aidan said quietly, sensing her hesitation.

Elora nodded, though she wasn't sure if she believed him. The road ahead was long, and the future was uncertain. But there was no turning back now.

Together, they stepped into the forest, leaving the sanctuary behind.

And with each step, Elora could feel the weight of her destiny pressing down on her, the power of the old gods thrumming beneath her skin.

The battle wasn't over.

It had only just begun.

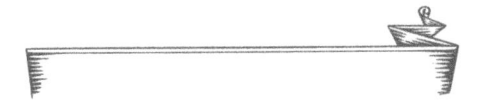

Chapter 8: The Path to the North

The road north was long and winding, cutting through dense forests and over jagged hills, every mile taking them farther from the safety of the sanctuary. As the sun climbed higher in the sky, its light filtering through the trees, Elora felt the weight of the journey settling on her shoulders. Each step forward was a reminder that the battle was not only for her own survival, but for the magic that held the world together.

The forest around them was alive with the sounds of rustling leaves and distant animal calls, yet Elora couldn't shake the sense of unease that clung to the air. The old ones had been beaten back, but she knew they were still out there, waiting. Watching. Their dark presence lingered in the corners of her mind, a constant, oppressive reminder that they would come again.

Aidan walked beside her, his face set in a grim expression as he scanned the path ahead. Lirael and Dorin followed closely, their senses alert to any signs of danger. Though the group had been traveling in relative silence, the unspoken tension hung heavy between them.

"We should reach the mountains by nightfall," Lirael said quietly, breaking the silence. "The sanctuary is hidden deep in a valley, away from prying eyes."

Elora nodded but didn't respond. Her mind was elsewhere, consumed by thoughts of the battle they had just left behind and the power she had unleashed. She had felt it stir within her again as they left the sanctuary—the power of the old gods, the magic that pulsed beneath her skin like a living thing. It was a part of her, but it was also something far greater, something ancient and dangerous.

And it terrified her.

Aidan glanced at her out of the corner of his eye, sensing her distraction. "You're quiet."

Elora forced a small smile. "Just thinking."

"About the old ones?" Aidan asked, his voice low.

"About everything," Elora admitted, her voice barely above a whisper. "The power I used back there... it was more than I ever expected. More than I ever wanted to use."

Aidan slowed his pace, his gaze softening as he turned to her. "You did what you had to do, Elora. You saved us."

"But at what cost?" Elora whispered, her throat tight. "The magic I carry... it's too much. If I keep using it like that, I don't know what will happen."

Aidan's face darkened. "You're stronger than you realize. And as long as you're in control, the power won't consume you."

Elora shook her head, her heart heavy with doubt. "That's the problem. I'm not sure I can control it anymore. Not with the old ones getting stronger."

Aidan stopped walking and placed a hand on her arm, his touch grounding her. "You don't have to do this alone, Elora. We're with you. And when the time comes, we'll fight together."

Elora looked into his eyes, seeing the unwavering resolve there, but also something else—something deeper. She could feel the bond between them, one that had been forged over centuries of shared battles and quiet moments. Aidan had always been there, even when she had pushed him away, even when the weight of her power and her immortality had driven a wedge between them.

"We'll figure this out," Aidan said softly. "But you need to trust yourself."

Elora's heart ached at his words. She had spent so long avoiding this, avoiding him. But now, with the world hanging in the balance, she had no choice but to face the truth.

"I trust you," Elora whispered, her voice barely audible.

For a moment, they stood in the middle of the forest, the world around them fading into the background. The connection between them hummed in the air, a fragile thread that had never truly been broken. Aidan's hand tightened on her arm, and Elora felt a flicker of warmth, of hope, in the midst of the darkness that surrounded them.

But the moment was shattered by the sound of rustling leaves nearby.

Aidan's grip on her arm tightened, and he spun around, drawing his sword in one fluid motion. Lirael and Dorin were at his side in an instant, their magic already sparking to life as they scanned the trees for any sign of danger.

"Elora," Lirael said sharply, her eyes darting through the shadows. "Do you feel that?"

Elora reached out with her senses, her heart racing. At first, there was nothing—just the familiar pulse of the earth beneath her feet, the steady hum of life all around them. But then, in the distance, she felt it. A dark, creeping presence. A cold wave of magic that sent a chill down her spine.

"They're here," Elora whispered, her voice tight with fear.

Aidan's face hardened, and he took a step forward, his eyes scanning the trees. "Stay close. We can't afford to get separated."

The dark presence grew stronger, the air around them growing colder as the old ones' magic seeped into the forest like a creeping fog. Elora's heart raced as she felt the familiar pull—the hunger of the old ones, their need to consume the magic she carried. They were drawn to her, their dark power reaching out, trying to ensnare her.

"We have to keep moving," Lirael said, her voice low but urgent. "If we stay here, they'll surround us."

Aidan nodded, motioning for them to follow. "Stay close."

The group moved swiftly through the trees, their footsteps barely making a sound as they pressed deeper into the forest. The dark presence followed them, growing stronger with each passing moment, the oppressive weight of the old ones' magic pressing against Elora's mind like a vice. She could feel them closing in, their power clawing at the edges of her consciousness, trying to drag her down.

Suddenly, the forest erupted in a wave of dark energy. The trees around them shuddered, the ground trembling beneath their feet as shadows twisted and writhed in the air. Dark figures emerged from the trees—twisted, smoke-like beings with glowing eyes that burned with an unnatural light.

"They've found us!" Dorin shouted, his voice filled with urgency.

Lirael's hands ignited with magic, her silver hair crackling with energy as she summoned a shield around them. "We need to break through!"

Elora's heart pounded as she watched the dark figures close in. The old ones' magic pulsed in the air, thick and suffocating, and she could feel the familiar pull—the power inside her responding to the threat, pushing her to unleash it once more.

But she couldn't. Not again. Not here.

Aidan swung his sword in a wide arc, cutting through one of the shadowy figures as it lunged at them, but more took its place, their twisted forms writhing in the air as they advanced.

"Elora!" Aidan shouted, his voice filled with urgency. "We need you!"

Elora's hands trembled as the power surged within her, threatening to break free. She had to do something. She had to protect them. But the fear gnawed at her—the fear of what might happen if she let go, if she unleashed the full force of her magic.

I can't lose control.

But as the dark figures closed in, their eyes glowing with hunger, Elora knew she had no choice. She couldn't hold back anymore.

With a deep breath, Elora raised her hands, feeling the magic roar to life inside her. The air around her crackled with energy as the earth responded, the pulse of the old gods' power surging through her veins.

The ground beneath her feet trembled, and the trees around them shook as Elora unleashed a wave of magic, a blinding light that tore through the shadows. The dark figures recoiled, their forms dissolving into smoke as the magic engulfed them.

The air was filled with the sound of crackling energy, the power of the old gods coursing through the forest like a storm. The shadows twisted and writhed, but they couldn't withstand the force of Elora's magic. One by one, they were torn apart, their dark forms dissolving into nothingness as the light consumed them.

And then, as quickly as it had begun, the forest fell silent.

Elora stood in the center of it all, her chest heaving, her hands still trembling with the remnants of her power. The dark presence was gone, the shadows banished. But the weight of what she had done still pressed down on her, heavy and suffocating.

Aidan approached her slowly, his sword still in hand, his eyes wide with a mixture of awe and concern. "Elora... are you all right?"

Elora nodded, though she wasn't sure if she was telling the truth. The power inside her had quieted, but it still hummed beneath the surface, waiting, watching.

"We need to keep moving," Lirael said, her voice tight with urgency. "They'll send more."

Elora took a deep breath, steadying herself. "Let's go."

Without another word, the group pressed forward, leaving the shadows behind.

But as they moved deeper into the forest, Elora couldn't shake the feeling that the old ones were still watching, waiting for the next chance to strike.

And the next time, she wasn't sure if she could stop them.

Chapter 9: Into the Depths of Fear

The forest felt like it was closing in as they moved deeper into the wilderness. The trees, once towering guardians of the ancient magic, now seemed ominous, their twisted branches casting long shadows on the path. The light of the sun barely reached them, blocked out by the thick canopy above, and the air was heavy with tension. Every step forward felt like it brought them closer to something dark and inevitable, a presence lurking just out of sight.

Elora kept her gaze focused ahead, her senses on high alert. The power she had unleashed still hummed beneath her skin, a reminder of the strength she carried, but also of the danger it posed. She had saved them, yes, but each time she tapped into that power, she felt herself slipping further from control. The old gods' magic was vast and unruly, and she feared what might happen if she couldn't contain it.

Aidan walked beside her, silent but watchful, his sword ready in case the shadows returned. Lirael and Dorin brought up the rear, their magic humming just beneath the surface, prepared for another attack. The weight of the journey pressed down on all of them, and though none spoke, Elora could feel the fear creeping in, the realization that they were up against something far greater than any of them had imagined.

The old ones weren't just powerful—they were relentless.

"Do you think they'll come back tonight?" Lirael asked quietly, her voice barely cutting through the tension-filled air.

"They will," Elora replied, her voice steady, though her heart pounded with dread. "They're not done. They'll keep coming."

Lirael nodded, though her expression was grim. "We need to reach the sanctuary before nightfall. It's the only place where the magic is strong enough to hold them back."

"How far are we?" Aidan asked, his eyes scanning the trees for any sign of movement.

"We're close," Lirael answered. "Another hour, maybe less. But we'll have to move quickly."

Elora's mind raced as they quickened their pace, the forest blurring around them. The sanctuary was their best hope, but even there, she knew it wouldn't be enough. The old ones were getting stronger, their hunger for the magic of the earth growing with each passing day. And they had tasted her power now. They wouldn't stop until they had taken it.

As they pressed on, the air grew colder, a biting chill that seemed to seep into Elora's bones. The path became more treacherous, the ground uneven and littered with rocks and roots that threatened to trip them at every turn. The trees pressed closer, their branches twisted and gnarled, casting dark shadows that seemed to flicker with movement.

Elora's heart raced as she felt the familiar presence of the old ones creeping in, their dark magic like a whisper in the back of her mind. They were watching, waiting, their hunger palpable. She could feel their eyes on her, could sense their twisted power reaching for her, trying to pull her in.

"We need to hurry," Dorin said, his voice tense. "They're getting closer."

Elora nodded, pushing herself forward, though the weight of the old ones' magic pressed down on her like a suffocating blanket. The forest seemed to darken around them, the shadows growing longer, deeper, as the presence of the old ones became more tangible. It was as if the forest itself was being swallowed by their dark power.

Suddenly, the ground beneath them trembled, a low rumble that sent a wave of unease through the group. The air grew colder still, and Elora felt the unmistakable pulse of dark magic surging through the earth.

"They're here," Aidan said, his voice tight with urgency.

Without warning, the forest erupted into chaos.

Dark figures emerged from the shadows, their twisted forms writhing like smoke as they surrounded the group. Their eyes glowed with an unnatural light, their movements slow but deliberate, as if savoring the fear that radiated from their prey. The air was thick with the oppressive weight of their magic, a dark, suffocating force that made it hard to breathe.

"Get ready!" Lirael shouted, her hands igniting with magic as she summoned a shield around them. The air crackled with energy as her power flared to life, a brilliant light cutting through the darkness.

Aidan drew his sword, his face set in grim determination as he moved to stand in front of Elora. "Stay close," he said, his voice low but firm.

Elora's heart pounded in her chest as she felt the dark presence pressing in, the old ones' magic wrapping around her like a noose. The familiar pull of their power tugged at her, urging her to fight, to unleash the magic inside her once more.

But she couldn't—she wouldn't.

She had to stay in control. She couldn't let the power consume her again.

The old ones moved closer, their forms twisting and shifting like shadows in the wind. They hissed and snarled, their dark energy spreading through the forest, corrupting everything it touched. The ground beneath their feet withered, the trees shuddered, and the air grew thick with the stench of decay.

"We have to break through!" Dorin shouted, his fists crackling with magic as he prepared to strike.

Lirael nodded, her silver hair glowing as she channeled her power into the shield. "Elora, can you—"

Before she could finish, the old ones attacked.

They moved with a speed and ferocity that caught the group off guard, their dark forms lunging at the shield with a force that sent cracks splintering through the protective barrier. The air was filled with the sound of hissing and snarling as the old ones' magic clashed with Lirael's light, the dark and the light battling for dominance.

Aidan swung his sword in wide, controlled arcs, cutting through the shadowy figures as they lunged at him. Dorin struck with his fists, sending bursts of magic through the air as he fought to keep the old ones at bay.

But there were too many.

Elora's breath came in ragged gasps as the dark magic pressed in on her, suffocating her, pulling at her. The power inside her stirred in response, pushing to be released, but Elora fought it down, her hands shaking as she struggled to keep control.

"I can't hold them back much longer!" Lirael shouted, her voice strained as the cracks in the shield grew larger, the old ones' magic seeping through.

Elora's chest tightened, the fear clawing at her throat. She couldn't let this happen. She couldn't let them take the magic.

But the old ones were relentless. Their hunger was insatiable, their dark power pushing harder, trying to break through, trying to take what was hers.

A dark figure lunged at her, its glowing eyes filled with hunger, its twisted form moving faster than she could react. Aidan saw it coming, but he was too far away. The figure reached for her, its hand outstretched, its magic wrapping around her like a vice, and for a moment, Elora felt the world close in around her.

And then, without thinking, she let go.

The power inside her erupted with a force so strong it knocked the figure back, sending a wave of light and energy surging through the clearing. The old ones recoiled, their dark forms dissolving into smoke as the magic tore through them, the light burning away the shadows.

Elora stood in the center of it all, her hands glowing with the raw, untamed power of the old gods. The earth beneath her feet pulsed with life, the ground cracking as the magic surged through her, wild and uncontrollable. The air crackled with energy, and the forest around them seemed to come alive, the trees shaking, the wind howling as the power swept through the clearing.

The old ones screamed, their twisted forms dissolving into nothingness as the light consumed them. The air was filled with the sound of crackling energy, the dark magic shattered by the force of Elora's power.

And then, as quickly as it had begun, the forest fell silent.

Elora stood trembling, her hands still glowing faintly with the remnants of her magic. The dark presence was gone, the old ones defeated—for now. But the weight of what she had done settled over her like a heavy cloak, the realization of her loss of control sinking in.

She had unleashed the power again. And once more, it had almost consumed her.

"Elora..." Aidan's voice was soft, filled with concern as he approached her. "Are you all right?"

Elora nodded, though her mind was racing. She had saved them again, but at what cost? Each time she used the power, it felt as though she was losing a piece of herself, losing her ability to control it.

"We need to keep moving," Lirael said, her voice tight with urgency. "There will be more."

Elora took a deep breath, steadying herself. "Let's go."

Without another word, the group pressed forward, leaving the shadows behind.

But Elora couldn't shake the feeling that something had shifted inside her. The power of the old gods was growing stronger, harder to contain.

And the next time, she wasn't sure if she could hold it back.

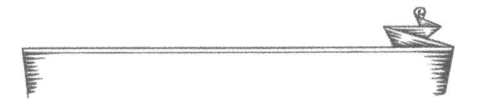

Chapter 10: The Sanctuary's Secret

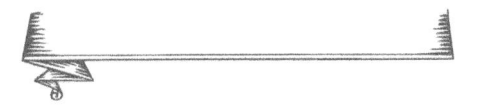

The sanctuary loomed before them, an imposing structure that had once radiated protection and power. Now, it felt cold and hollow, the runes barely flickering with the magic that had once made this place sacred. Elora could feel the emptiness in the air, the pull of dark magic lingering like a scar. The old ones had been here—there was no mistaking their presence.

"They've drained the magic," Lirael said softly, her silver hair whipping in the cold wind as she stared at the darkened walls. "The sanctuary is dying."

Elora's heart clenched at the words. This place, once a stronghold of the old ways, was now a shadow of what it had been. The old ones were methodical, like predators slowly stripping the world of its defenses. They were hunting the very magic that sustained the earth, and the sanctuary had been a prime target.

Aidan stepped forward, his eyes scanning the area, his expression grim. "They might still be here. We should be careful."

Dorin nodded in agreement, his fists crackling with faint traces of magic, ready for a fight. "If they left anything behind, we need to know. They may have left clues."

Elora remained silent, the unease inside her growing. She could still feel the traces of the old ones' power, like a distant echo vibrating through the ground. It wasn't just that they had drained the sanctuary of its magic—there was something deeper, something buried in this place. A secret she could sense but not yet fully understand.

"We need to go inside," Elora said, her voice quiet but firm. "There might still be something left. Something that can help us."

Lirael hesitated, glancing at the others before nodding. "The magic here is weak, but you're right. The sanctuary was built to protect. There may still be wards that can guide us."

With cautious steps, the group made their way toward the sanctuary's entrance, the heavy stone doors standing ajar as if left in a hurry. The air grew colder as they approached, the remnants of the old ones' magic clinging to the stone walls like a sickness. Each step sent a shiver down Elora's spine, the power inside her stirring in response to the dark energy that surrounded them.

As they stepped inside, the cold seemed to deepen, and the air became thicker, heavier. The sanctuary's once grand hallways were dim, the faint glow of ancient runes barely illuminating the path ahead. Dust hung in the air, and the echoes of their footsteps reverberated against the walls, making the place feel more like a tomb than a refuge.

Elora's hand brushed the wall, her fingers tracing the faint glow of the runes. She could feel the magic still lingering here, but it was weak—fading. The sanctuary had been drained almost completely, but not everything had been lost.

"There's still something here," Elora whispered, her voice echoing in the vast, empty space. "The magic hasn't completely disappeared."

Aidan glanced at her, his eyes narrowing. "You think the old ones missed something?"

"Maybe," Elora said softly, her fingers still trailing along the runes. "Or maybe there's something they couldn't reach."

Lirael stepped forward, her hand resting on the hilt of her blade as she scanned the room. "We should split up. If there's anything left, we need to find it before they come back."

Dorin nodded, his expression hard. "We'll take the west wing. Aidan, Elora—you take the east."

Elora hesitated, glancing at Aidan before nodding. The old ones' presence still lingered here, and she could feel the weight of their power pressing down on her. But there was something else, something deeper, that called to her. She wasn't sure if it was the sanctuary's magic or the pull of the old gods' power within her, but she knew they had to search.

Aidan led the way, his sword drawn as they moved deeper into the sanctuary. The air grew colder, the walls narrowing as they entered the east wing. The flickering glow of the runes barely provided enough light to see, and the oppressive weight of the old ones' magic seemed to press down harder with each step.

"We're getting closer," Aidan said, his voice low. "I can feel it."

Elora nodded, though her chest tightened with each step. The power inside her responded to the darkness around them, the magic of the old gods stirring as if in warning. She had to be careful—if the old ones were still here, they would be drawn to the power she carried.

The hallway opened into a vast chamber, its walls lined with ancient carvings and more faintly glowing runes. At the center of the room stood a massive stone altar, its surface etched with intricate patterns that shimmered faintly in the dim light.

But the room wasn't empty.

Elora's breath caught in her throat as she saw the figure standing at the altar, their back turned to them. The figure was cloaked in shadow, their presence dark and oppressive, the air around them crackling with energy. There was no mistaking the power that radiated from them—it was the same dark magic she had felt during their battles with the old ones.

Aidan stiffened beside her, his grip tightening on his sword as he took a step forward. "Who are you?"

The figure didn't move, but Elora could feel their attention shift, their focus now entirely on her. The air grew colder, the magic swirling around them intensifying as the figure finally turned to face them.

It was a woman, her face pale and angular, her eyes burning with a strange, eerie light. She was beautiful in a way that was unsettling, her features sharp and otherworldly, her dark hair cascading down her back like a river of shadows. But it was the power that radiated from her that held Elora's attention—the same twisted, hungry magic of the old ones.

"You've come for answers," the woman said, her voice smooth and melodic, though it sent a shiver down Elora's spine. "But you won't find them here."

THE ETERNAL CIRCLE

Aidan stepped in front of Elora, his sword raised. "Who are you?"

The woman smiled, but there was no warmth in it. "I am something you cannot comprehend. But you know me, Elora. You've felt me before."

Elora's heart pounded in her chest as she met the woman's gaze, her mind racing. There was something familiar about her—something ancient and dark, something that tugged at the edges of her memory.

"You're one of them," Elora whispered, her voice trembling. "One of the old ones."

The woman's smile widened. "I am more than that. I am the beginning and the end, the shadow that has always followed you. The power you carry—it belongs to me."

Elora took a step back, her body trembling as the full weight of the woman's presence pressed down on her. The power inside her surged, responding to the threat, and she struggled to keep it under control.

"You'll never take it," Aidan growled, his sword flashing in the dim light as he stepped toward the woman.

The woman's eyes flickered with amusement, but she didn't move. "I don't need to take it. The power inside her will destroy her on its own. And when it does, I will be there to claim what's left."

Elora's hands trembled, her heart racing as she felt the power inside her stir, pushing against the barriers she had so carefully constructed. The woman's words cut deep, echoing the fear she had carried for so long—that the power of the old gods was too much for her to control, that it would consume her in the end.

But she couldn't let that happen. She wouldn't.

"You're wrong," Elora said, her voice steadying despite the fear that gnawed at her. "I control the power, not the other way around."

The woman's smile faded, her eyes narrowing. "Do you, Elora? Or is it already controlling you?"

The air crackled with energy as the woman raised her hand, dark magic swirling around her like a storm. Aidan tensed, ready to strike, but Elora raised a hand to stop him.

This was her fight.

The power inside her surged again, and this time, she didn't push it down. She let it rise, let it fill her, but she kept a tight grip on it, refusing to let it slip out of her control. The air around her crackled with energy as the magic of the old gods pulsed through her veins, and the ground beneath her feet trembled in response.

The woman's eyes gleamed with interest, her lips curling into a wicked smile. "Ah, there it is. The power I've been waiting for."

Elora took a deep breath, grounding herself as the magic surged through her. She had spent centuries running from this, but now, standing face to face with one of the old ones, she knew she couldn't run anymore. The power inside her wasn't a curse—it was a gift, one she had been given to protect the earth and its magic.

She wouldn't let the old ones take it. Not now. Not ever.

With a single, determined thought, Elora unleashed her power.

The room exploded with light, the air filled with the sound of crackling energy as the magic of the old gods surged through her, brighter and stronger than ever before. The ground shook, the ancient runes on the walls flaring to life as the sanctuary responded to the power she wielded.

The woman's smile vanished, her eyes wide with shock as the light engulfed her. The dark magic that had surrounded her faltered, crumbling under the weight of Elora's power.

For a moment, the air was filled with the clash of light and darkness, the magic of the old gods battling against the twisted power of the old ones. And then, with a deafening roar, the dark magic shattered, and the woman vanished, consumed by the light.

Silence fell over the chamber.

Elora stood in the center of it all, her chest heaving, her hands still glowing with the remnants of her magic. The power inside her had quieted, but it was still there, humming beneath the surface, waiting.

Aidan lowered his sword, his eyes wide with awe as he stepped toward her. "Elora... you did it."

Elora nodded, though the weight of what she had just done still pressed down on her. She had defeated the woman, but the old ones weren't gone. They would come again.

But for now, they had won.

Lirael and Dorin appeared in the doorway, their eyes wide with shock as they took in the scene. "What happened?" Dorin asked, his voice filled with disbelief.

"Elora happened," Aidan said, his voice filled with quiet admiration.

Elora took a deep breath, steadying herself as the remnants of her power faded. She had done it. She had controlled the magic. But as the others gathered around her, the weight of her responsibility settled over her once more.

This was only the beginning.

The old ones would come again, and when they did, they would be stronger.

But Elora would be ready.

She had to be.

Chapter 11: A Fragile Victory

The aftermath of the battle lingered in the sanctuary, the air still thick with the remnants of Elora's unleashed power. The chamber was quiet now, the faint hum of magic a stark contrast to the chaos that had raged only moments before. The walls, once dim and lifeless, now glowed faintly, the ancient runes flickering with renewed life. But despite the calm that had settled over the space, Elora could feel the weight of what had just transpired pressing down on her, like a heavy shroud that refused to lift.

Her chest rose and fell with each labored breath, her hands still trembling from the intensity of the magic she had called forth. The power of the old gods had surged through her with a ferocity that had left her shaken to her core. It had been so close to overwhelming her, to tearing her apart from the inside out. But somehow, she had held on. Somehow, she had controlled it—just barely.

Aidan stood beside her, his sword lowered, his eyes filled with concern. He hadn't spoken since the battle had ended, but his gaze never left her, as if he feared she might collapse at any moment. His hand hovered near her arm, hesitant, as if unsure whether to reach out to her or to keep his distance.

"Elora," he said softly, his voice barely above a whisper, "are you all right?"

Elora nodded, though the truth was far more complicated than she was willing to admit. She felt hollow, drained, as if the magic had taken more from her than just her strength. There was a fragility in her now, a sense that something within her had shifted, had broken. But she couldn't afford to show weakness. Not now. Not with the old ones still lurking in the shadows, waiting for their next chance to strike.

"I'm fine," she lied, her voice steadier than she felt.

Aidan frowned, his eyes searching hers, but he didn't push. He knew her well enough to sense when she wasn't telling the whole truth, but he also knew when to let it go.

Lirael and Dorin approached slowly, their faces pale, their expressions a mixture of awe and uncertainty. The glow of the runes reflected off Lirael's silver hair, casting a soft light across her face as she surveyed the room. The tension in the air was palpable, thick with unspoken questions and doubts.

"What happened?" Lirael asked, her voice soft but firm, breaking the silence that had settled over them.

Elora took a deep breath, her gaze drifting to the spot where the old one had stood. There was no trace of her now, no lingering presence of the dark magic that had filled the chamber. The woman had vanished, consumed by the light of Elora's power, but the threat she posed still loomed large in Elora's mind.

"She's gone," Elora said quietly, though the words felt hollow in her mouth. "But she wasn't the last."

Dorin's brow furrowed, his broad shoulders tensing as he took in the gravity of her words. "If there are more like her out there, we're going to need more than just this sanctuary to stop them."

Elora nodded, her heart heavy with the truth. The old ones weren't finished. This victory, if it could even be called that, was fragile at best. The woman had spoken of the power inside Elora as if it were already slipping away from her, as if the old ones had some plan to use it against her. That thought gnawed at the edges of her mind, a dark cloud she couldn't shake.

"There are more sanctuaries," Lirael said, her voice filled with quiet determination. "Scattered across the land. We need to find them, to rally anyone who remembers the old magic. We can't face this alone."

Elora turned to Lirael, her thoughts swirling. She wanted to believe in the sanctuaries, in the hope that there were still places in the world where the old magic remained strong. But after seeing how easily this sanctuary had been drained, how the runes had flickered and died under the weight of the old ones' power, she wasn't sure how much faith she could place in them.

"Their magic is getting stronger," Elora said, her voice tight with frustration. "They're draining the earth, taking its power for themselves. If we don't find a way to stop them, no sanctuary will be safe."

A heavy silence followed her words, the weight of their situation settling over them like a storm cloud. Dorin ran a hand through his hair, his expression dark with thought. "We can't just run. We need a plan."

Elora's mind raced, her thoughts returning to the moment when she had faced the old one in the chamber. There had been something in the woman's eyes—something beyond hunger, beyond malice. She had seemed almost... curious. As if she had been studying Elora, waiting for her to lose control. And that unsettled her more than the battle itself.

"She said the power would destroy me," Elora said, her voice low but clear. "That it's already consuming me."

Aidan's gaze snapped to hers, his expression sharp. "You can't listen to her. She wanted to weaken you, to make you doubt yourself."

Elora met his gaze, but the doubt had already taken root. She could feel it growing inside her, feeding on her fear. She had felt the power slipping through her fingers during the battle, the way it had threatened to overwhelm her. And it terrified her.

"We can't ignore what she said," Lirael said carefully, her voice soft but firm. "If the old ones know something about the power you carry, we need to understand it. We need to find out what they're planning."

Elora's heart sank. The thought of confronting that part of herself—the part tied to the old gods, to the ancient magic that had been buried inside her for centuries—was something she had spent her entire life avoiding. But now, it seemed, she had no choice.

"There must be records," Dorin suggested, his voice filled with a kind of reluctant hope. "In the old texts, the ancient scrolls. Something that can tell us how to fight them."

Lirael nodded, her face set with determination. "The sanctuaries were built to preserve that knowledge. If there's anything that can help us, we'll find it."

Elora closed her eyes for a moment, letting the weight of the conversation wash over her. She knew they were right. They

THE ETERNAL CIRCLE

needed answers—answers about the old ones, about the power she carried, and about how to stop them before the world was consumed by darkness. But the path ahead was uncertain, and each step seemed more dangerous than the last.

"We'll start with the sanctuaries," Elora said finally, her voice steady. "But we need to move quickly. Every day we lose is another step closer to the old ones taking the earth's magic."

Aidan nodded, his expression resolute. "Then we leave at first light."

As the group began to disperse, each heading off to prepare for the journey ahead, Elora remained in the center of the chamber, her eyes lingering on the runes that flickered faintly on the walls. The sanctuary had been drained, but the magic hadn't died completely. There was still life here, still hope.

But as she stood alone in the dim light, the silence of the chamber pressing in around her, Elora couldn't shake the feeling that their victory was fleeting, that the old ones were closer than ever. They had won this battle, but the war was far from over.

Her hands trembled as she ran them over the smooth stone of the altar, the weight of the magic still buzzing beneath her skin. The power of the old gods was hers to wield, but it came with a cost—a cost she wasn't sure she could bear.

The woman's words echoed in her mind, a quiet taunt that refused to fade.

The power will destroy you.

Elora closed her eyes, taking a deep breath as she steadied herself. She couldn't afford to doubt. Not now. The fate of the world rested on her shoulders, and she would carry that burden, no matter the cost.

But as she opened her eyes and looked out at the darkened sanctuary, she knew that their fragile victory was only the beginning.

And the real battle was yet to come.

Elora made her way to the small, secluded alcove at the back of the sanctuary, her footsteps echoing faintly against the stone floor. The others were busy preparing for the next leg of their journey, but she needed a moment to herself, a moment to process everything that had happened.

As she entered the alcove, she let out a slow, measured breath, her shoulders sagging under the weight of her exhaustion. She had held herself together in front of the others, but now, in the quiet solitude of the sanctuary, the full impact of the battle hit her like a tidal wave. Her hands shook as she sank to her knees, her body trembling from the aftershocks of the power she had wielded.

The magic still hummed inside her, a living, breathing force that refused to be tamed. It was stronger now, more insistent, pushing at the edges of her control. She could feel it pressing against her mind, whispering to her, urging her to let go, to give in to its strength.

But she couldn't.

Not now. Not ever.

Elora closed her eyes, focusing on her breath, trying to ground herself. She had always feared this moment—the moment when the power would become too much, when she would lose control and the magic would consume her. But now, with the old ones closing in, that fear had become all too real.

Her fingers dug into the stone floor as she fought to steady herself, to regain control. She had faced the old ones, had stood against their darkness, but at what cost? The woman's words echoed in her mind, a constant reminder of the danger she faced.

The power will destroy you.

Elora opened her eyes, staring at the faint glow of the runes on the wall. She wouldn't let that happen. She couldn't. The earth's magic depended on her, on the strength she carried. But as the shadows of the old ones loomed larger, she knew the path ahead would only grow more treacherous.

With a deep breath, Elora rose to her feet, her hands still shaking but her resolve firm. The war was far from over, and the old ones would not rest until they had taken everything.

But neither would she.

Elora stepped out of the alcove, her eyes set on the horizon. The power of the old gods was hers to control, and she would fight to protect the world she loved, even if it meant losing herself in the process.

For now, their victory was fragile. But the real battle was just beginning.

And Elora would be ready.

Chapter 12: The Path of Sacrifice

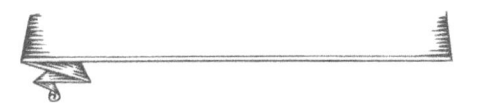

The dawn was a pale streak across the horizon, casting a cold, silvery light over the sanctuary. The group gathered at the edge of the valley, preparing to leave behind the ruins of their temporary victory. The air was still, and the weight of the battle clung to them like a shadow. Elora stood slightly apart from the others, her gaze fixed on the distant mountains, where the next sanctuary waited—if it still stood.

Her body still ached from the aftermath of the magic she had unleashed, but it was the deeper pain, the one in her chest, that weighed most heavily on her. The fragile victory they had won here felt hollow, a fleeting triumph in the face of an enemy that grew stronger with each passing day.

Aidan approached quietly, his presence familiar and steady. He didn't speak for a moment, standing beside her as they both watched the horizon. The unspoken tension between them was thick—Aidan had always known when to push her and when to let her be. But now, it felt as though even he was unsure of what to say.

Finally, he broke the silence. "You've been quiet."

Elora didn't turn to face him, her gaze still focused on the mountains. "I'm trying to figure out how much time we have before they find us again."

Aidan exhaled softly, his breath visible in the cool morning air. "Not much, I'd guess."

She nodded. The old ones wouldn't stay away for long. Their hunger for the power she carried would draw them back, and they would be even more dangerous the next time they came. That thought gnawed at her, feeding the growing fear that she was running out of options—and time.

"You did well," Aidan said after a moment, his voice low but sincere. "You stopped her. You controlled it."

Elora finally turned to look at him, her eyes searching his for any sign of doubt. But all she saw was the quiet faith he had always had in her, even when she didn't believe in herself. "I nearly lost control."

"But you didn't," Aidan said firmly. "You held on."

Elora clenched her fists at her sides, frustration boiling up inside her. "I can't keep doing this. Every time I use the power, it's harder to control. I don't know how long I can keep it from... from consuming me."

Aidan's expression softened, and he reached out, his hand brushing against her arm. "You won't let it."

Her heart twisted at his certainty, at the quiet conviction in his voice. She wished she could share his faith, but the truth was that the magic of the old gods was too powerful, too wild. Every time she called on it, she felt a piece of herself slipping away, lost in the overwhelming tide of energy that surged through her.

"You don't understand," Elora said quietly, her voice trembling with the weight of her fear. "The old ones aren't just coming for the magic. They're coming for me."

Aidan's brow furrowed, his eyes darkening with concern. "What do you mean?"

Elora took a deep breath, her gaze drifting to the distant mountains once more. "The woman I fought—she said the power inside me is already destroying me. She was... watching, waiting for me to lose control. And when I did, she planned to take what was left."

Aidan's grip on her arm tightened slightly. "She was trying to manipulate you, Elora. To weaken your resolve."

Elora shook her head. "No, it was more than that. She knew something. She knew that the power of the old gods... it's not just a gift. It's a curse."

The silence that followed her words was heavy, and for a moment, neither of them spoke. Aidan's hand fell away from her arm, and his expression turned grim.

"What do you want to do?" he asked softly.

Elora didn't answer right away. She didn't know what to do. Every instinct told her to keep fighting, to push forward, to find a way to stop the old ones before it was too late. But the weight of the power she carried was growing heavier with each passing day, and she feared that one day soon, she wouldn't be able to bear it any longer.

"I don't know," she admitted, her voice barely above a whisper. "I just know that the more I use the magic, the more I lose myself to it. And if I can't stop them before that happens..."

Aidan's gaze softened, his concern deepening. "You're not alone in this, Elora. We'll figure it out. We'll find a way."

She wanted to believe him. She wanted to believe that there was a way out of this, a way to stop the old ones without sacrificing herself in the process. But deep down, she feared that the only way to win was to give in to the magic completely—and that meant losing herself forever.

"Ready?" Lirael's voice broke through the silence, and Elora turned to see the others gathering near the edge of the valley, their packs slung over their shoulders, their faces set with grim determination.

Elora nodded, though the weight of uncertainty still pressed down on her. "We're ready."

As the group began their journey toward the mountains, the silence between them felt heavier than before. Elora kept her gaze focused ahead, her thoughts swirling with the dark possibilities of what lay ahead.

The path was steep and unforgiving, the terrain growing rougher as they climbed higher into the mountains. The air grew colder, the wind biting at their skin, but none of them slowed. There was a sense of urgency in every step, as if they could feel the old ones closing in behind them.

Hours passed in silence, the sound of their footsteps the only noise cutting through the stillness. Elora's mind drifted as they walked, her thoughts consumed by the power she carried and the fear of what it might do to her. The memory of the battle in the sanctuary played over and over in her mind—the surge of magic, the way it had nearly overwhelmed her, the way she had almost lost control.

It was terrifying.

"Elora," Lirael's voice cut through her thoughts, pulling her back to the present. "We're close."

Elora blinked, realizing that they had reached the top of a ridge. Below them, nestled deep in the mountains, was the next sanctuary—a sprawling complex of stone buildings, surrounded by towering cliffs and dense forest. From this distance, it looked peaceful, untouched.

But Elora could feel it.

The same dark presence that had tainted the first sanctuary lingered here. The old ones had been here. The air was heavy with the remnants of their magic, like a wound that hadn't fully healed.

"They've already been here," Elora said quietly, her heart sinking.

Aidan frowned, scanning the valley below. "How bad do you think it is?"

Elora closed her eyes for a moment, reaching out with her senses. The magic here was faint, weak, but it was still there. It hadn't been completely drained, not yet. But it was only a matter of time.

"We need to move quickly," she said, her voice steady. "If there's anything left, we have to find it before they come back."

The group descended the ridge in silence, the weight of their mission pressing down on them. As they approached the sanctuary, the full extent of the damage became clear. The buildings were intact, but the runes that had once protected the place were dim, their glow barely visible in the fading light. The air was thick with the stench of decay, the ground blackened in places where the old ones' magic had touched it.

Elora's heart sank as they stepped through the entrance, the silence inside the sanctuary deafening. It was as if the very life had been drained from the place, leaving only a hollow shell behind.

"There's still magic here," Lirael said, her voice quiet as she ran her hand over one of the faded runes. "But it's fading."

Elora nodded, her senses tingling with the remnants of the old ones' power. They had been here, but they hadn't finished what they started. There was still time, but not much.

"We need to find the archives," Dorin said, his voice tense. "If there's any information about the old ones or the power they're after, it'll be there."

The group moved deeper into the sanctuary, their footsteps echoing off the stone walls as they made their way toward the inner chambers. Elora's heart pounded in her chest, her mind racing with the fear that they were already too late, that the old ones had taken everything.

As they entered the archives, Elora's breath caught in her throat. The room was vast, lined with shelves of ancient scrolls and tomes, their pages glowing faintly with the remnants of magic. But many of the shelves were empty, the scrolls that had once been there now gone, likely destroyed or taken by the old ones.

"They've already started," Lirael whispered, her face pale as she surveyed the room.

Elora's heart sank. The knowledge they needed, the secrets that could help them stop the old ones, might already be lost. But there had to be something left, something they could use.

"We'll search," Elora said, her voice firm. "There has to be something here."

The group spread out, each of them scanning the shelves, searching through the remaining scrolls and tomes for any hint of information. Elora moved to the far side of the room, her fingers brushing against the fragile pages of an ancient book. The words were faded, written in a language she barely recognized, but the magic that pulsed from the pages was unmistakable.

She could feel it—a connection to the old gods, to the power she carried.

"Elora," Aidan called softly from across the room. "Over here."

She hurried over to where he stood, his hand resting on a small, weathered tome. The pages were brittle, but the writing was clear, etched with ancient runes and symbols that pulsed with faint magic.

"This might be it," Aidan said, his voice filled with hope.

Elora took the book from him, her heart racing as she carefully opened it. The writing was old, older than anything she had seen before, but it spoke of the old gods, of their power, and of a time before the old ones had been banished.

As she read, her blood ran cold.

The book didn't just speak of the old gods' power. It spoke of a price—a sacrifice that had to be made to keep the balance between light and dark. A sacrifice tied to the very magic she carried.

Elora's hands trembled as she read the final passage, her breath catching in her throat.

To wield the power of the old gods is to walk the path of sacrifice. Only in giving up the self can the magic be controlled. Only in surrendering everything can the balance be restored.

Her heart pounded in her chest as the full weight of the words settled over her.

She had been right. The power of the old gods wasn't just a gift—it was a curse.

And the only way to stop the old ones was to give up the very thing that had kept her alive for centuries.

Her immortality. Her life.

"Elora," Aidan's voice broke through her thoughts, his hand resting on her shoulder. "What is it?"

Elora closed the book slowly, her hands shaking as she met his gaze. "I know how to stop them," she whispered, her voice trembling with the weight of the truth. "But it's going to cost me everything."

Aidan's eyes widened, his face paling as the meaning of her words sank in. "No," he said, his voice filled with quiet desperation. "There has to be another way."

Elora shook her head, her heart heavy with the knowledge of what she had to do. "This is the only way, Aidan. The magic... it's tied to me. If I don't stop it, if I don't sacrifice myself, the old ones will take it. And then, they'll take the earth."

The silence that followed was suffocating, the weight of her words pressing down on both of them like a heavy blanket.

Aidan's hand tightened on her shoulder, his eyes filled with anguish. "We'll find another way," he said, his voice breaking. "There has to be another way."

Elora's heart twisted at the pain in his voice, but she knew the truth. There was no other way. The old ones were too strong, and the magic inside her was too dangerous. If she didn't stop them, the world would be consumed by darkness.

"I have to do this," Elora said softly, her voice filled with quiet resolve. "It's the only way."

Aidan's eyes searched hers, his face filled with desperation and fear. But in the end, he didn't argue. He knew as well as she did that there was no other choice.

They stood in silence, the weight of the sacrifice that lay ahead hanging heavy between them.

The path of sacrifice had always been her destiny.

And now, it was time to walk it.

Chapter 13: The Weight of Destiny

The silence stretched between Elora and Aidan, a fragile thread holding them both together and pulling them apart. The weight of her decision hung in the air like a dark cloud, suffocating in its finality. Elora could feel Aidan's anguish, the quiet desperation in his eyes as he tried to process the reality of what she had just said. But she knew there was no other way. The path of sacrifice had always been hers to walk.

The book she held felt impossibly heavy in her hands, the ancient words etched on its pages echoing in her mind. *Only in giving up the self can the magic be controlled. Only in surrendering everything can the balance be restored.* She had carried the power of the old gods for centuries, but now, she understood the truth. The magic wasn't meant to be wielded by one person forever. It had to be given up, surrendered, for the greater good.

"I can't let you do this," Aidan said finally, his voice rough with emotion. He stepped closer, his hand still on her shoulder, his eyes pleading. "There has to be another way, Elora. We've always found a way before."

Elora's heart ached at his words. She wished it could be different. She wished there was another solution, one that didn't involve her death. But the old ones were growing stronger, and the magic inside her was too dangerous to be left unchecked. If she didn't stop them, if she didn't make the ultimate sacrifice, the entire world would fall into darkness.

"There is no other way," Elora whispered, her voice barely audible over the sound of the wind that howled outside the sanctuary. "The power... it's connected to me. If I don't let go, they'll take it. And then nothing will stop them."

Aidan's hand tightened on her shoulder, his eyes filled with a mixture of anger and sorrow. "We'll fight them. Together. We don't need to sacrifice you. We'll find another way."

Elora shook her head, her heart breaking at the thought of leaving him behind. Aidan had been her constant through the centuries, her anchor in the storm of her immortality. But this wasn't a battle they could win through sheer force. This was about the magic, the ancient power that had been given to her by the old gods. And now, it had to be given up.

"I have to do this," Elora said, her voice stronger now, though it trembled with the weight of what she was saying. "It's my responsibility. It's why I was given this power in the first place. To protect the earth, to keep the balance. And the only way to do that now... is to let it go."

Aidan's face twisted in pain, his jaw clenched as he fought to hold back the torrent of emotions swirling inside him. He opened his mouth to speak, but no words came out. The silence that followed was unbearable, filled with the unspoken truth that both of them had known all along.

"You're not alone in this, Elora," Aidan said, his voice finally breaking through the silence. "I'm with you. No matter what."

Elora felt tears prick at the corners of her eyes, but she blinked them back. She couldn't afford to fall apart now. She had made her choice, and now she had to see it through.

"Thank you," she whispered, her voice thick with emotion. "But this is something I have to do alone."

Aidan's expression hardened, his eyes flashing with frustration. "No. I'm not letting you face this alone. I won't."

Before Elora could respond, Lirael and Dorin entered the room, their faces grim as they took in the tension that hung between her and Aidan. Lirael's sharp eyes flicked to the book in Elora's hands, and the faint glow of the ancient runes on the pages.

"Did you find something?" Lirael asked, though her tone suggested she already knew the answer.

Elora nodded slowly, her fingers tightening around the book. "I found out how to stop the old ones. But it requires... a sacrifice."

Lirael's eyes narrowed, her expression unreadable. "What kind of sacrifice?"

Elora hesitated, the weight of the truth pressing down on her chest like a stone. "The power I carry—it's tied to me. The only way to stop the old ones is to give it up. To surrender it."

Lirael's face paled as understanding dawned. "You mean... your life."

Elora nodded, her heart sinking as the words left her lips. The reality of her fate was sinking in now, and it felt heavier than ever. But there was no turning back.

"There must be another way," Dorin said, his voice filled with urgency. "This can't be the only solution."

Elora shook her head, her voice steady but filled with sorrow. "It's the only way. The power is too dangerous. If the old ones take it, the world will fall. The balance will be destroyed."

Lirael's expression softened, though her eyes were still filled with tension. "And you're willing to give up everything for this?"

Elora's gaze dropped to the floor. She had spent centuries guarding this power, protecting the earth and its magic. And now, she was faced with the one thing she had never truly prepared for—giving it all up.

"I have to," she whispered, the words barely audible. "It's my responsibility."

The room fell into silence again, the gravity of her words settling over them all like a suffocating blanket. Each of them knew the truth, but none of them wanted to face it. The path ahead was dark, and Elora could feel the weight of every step pulling her down.

Finally, Lirael stepped forward, her face set with quiet determination. "Then we'll help you. Whatever you need."

Elora looked up, surprised by the strength in Lirael's voice. She hadn't expected them to accept her decision so easily, but the truth was that they understood. They understood the cost, and they understood that this was the only way to save the world.

"We'll need to prepare," Lirael continued, her eyes scanning the room. "The old ones will come for you as soon as they sense what you're doing. We need to be ready for them."

Dorin nodded, his face grim. "We'll hold them off as long as we can."

THE ETERNAL CIRCLE

Elora's heart ached at the thought of her friends fighting for her, putting themselves in danger to protect her while she made the ultimate sacrifice. But she knew there was no other choice. This was the only way.

"We don't have much time," Elora said softly, her gaze drifting to the faint glow of the runes on the walls. "The old ones are already getting stronger. We need to do this soon."

Aidan stepped closer to her, his voice low and filled with emotion. "Are you sure?"

Elora met his gaze, her heart heavy with the knowledge of what lay ahead. "Yes," she whispered. "I'm sure."

The silence that followed was thick with unspoken emotion, but there was no more room for hesitation. They had to act.

Lirael and Dorin began to move, gathering what they needed to reinforce the sanctuary's defenses, while Aidan stayed by Elora's side, his eyes never leaving her. He didn't say anything, but Elora could feel the quiet devastation radiating off of him. He had always been her protector, the one constant in her long, immortal life. And now, she was leaving him behind.

As the others worked, Elora stepped outside, the cool mountain air brushing against her skin. She looked up at the sky, at the stars that blinked faintly in the predawn light. She had seen so many stars, so many nights like this one. But tonight felt different.

This was the beginning of the end.

Aidan joined her, standing beside her in the silence. He didn't speak, but his presence was enough. For a moment, they stood there together, the weight of their shared history hanging in the air between them.

"I'm sorry," Elora whispered, her voice barely audible over the wind.

Aidan turned to her, his expression filled with pain. "Don't be. You've spent your entire life protecting everyone else. Now it's time for us to protect you."

Elora's heart twisted at his words, and for a moment, she allowed herself to feel the full weight of her emotions. The fear, the sorrow, the love. She had lived for so long, had seen so much, but she had never been able to truly live. Always moving, always guarding, always carrying the burden of the old gods' power.

But now, she had a chance to end it. To finally stop running. To finally give the earth a chance to heal.

"I'll miss you," Aidan said, his voice breaking slightly. "I've always known you were stronger than all of us, but I never thought it would come to this."

Elora looked up at him, her eyes shining with unshed tears. "I'll miss you too."

Aidan stepped closer, his hand reaching for hers. Their fingers intertwined, and for a moment, the world seemed to fade away. There was nothing but the two of them, standing together in the quiet stillness of the mountain night.

And then, as the first light of dawn began to break over the horizon, Elora knew it was time.

She pulled away from Aidan, her heart heavy but her resolve strong. "We need to begin."

Aidan's eyes glistened, but he nodded, his jaw tight with the pain he couldn't put into words.

Together, they walked back inside, where Lirael and Dorin were waiting. The room was prepared, the runes glowing faintly as they cast their protective spells. The air was thick with tension, the weight of what was about to happen pressing down on them all.

Elora took her place at the center of the room, her heart pounding in her chest. She could feel the magic stirring inside her, waiting for her to release it, waiting for her to make the ultimate sacrifice.

Lirael stepped forward, her face pale but determined. "We'll protect you, Elora. We'll hold them off as long as we can."

Elora nodded, her throat tight. "Thank you."

The others took their positions, forming a protective circle around her. The air crackled with magic, the runes glowing brighter as the energy in the room built. Elora closed her eyes, her heart racing as she felt the power of the old gods rise within her.

This was it. This was the moment she had been dreading for centuries.

The power surged inside her, wild and untamed, and she fought to keep control as the magic swirled around her. She could feel the presence of the old ones growing closer, their dark magic pressing against the edges of the sanctuary. They knew what she was doing. They were coming for her.

But she couldn't stop now.

With a deep breath, Elora began the ritual, her voice steady as she spoke the ancient words. The room hummed with energy, the magic building to a crescendo as the power inside her reached its peak.

And then, with a final, shattering release, Elora let go.

The magic exploded outward, a blinding light filling the room as the power of the old gods was unleashed. The earth trembled beneath her, the air crackling with energy as the magic surged through her, wild and unstoppable.

The old ones' presence grew stronger, their dark magic pressing harder against the sanctuary's defenses. But Elora didn't falter. She kept going, her heart steady as the magic flowed through her, consuming her, piece by piece.

And then, in the final moments, as the light engulfed her, Elora felt a strange sense of peace.

She had done it.

She had saved the earth.

And as the world faded away, Elora knew that her sacrifice had been worth it.

The balance had been restored.

And her long journey had finally come to an end.

Chapter 14: The Echo of Her Power

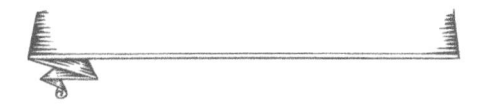

The aftermath of Elora's sacrifice lingered in the sanctuary like a ghost, the air still humming faintly with the remnants of her magic. The room was quiet now, the blinding light that had filled the space fading to a soft, glowing warmth. The runes on the walls flickered gently, their protective magic still in place, but the oppressive weight of the old ones' presence had lifted. The darkness that had loomed over them for so long had finally been pushed back.

But Elora was gone.

Aidan stood at the center of the room, staring at the spot where she had been only moments ago, his heart heavy with the loss. The others stood around him, their faces pale and drawn, their expressions a mixture of sorrow and disbelief. No one spoke. There was nothing to say.

The magic of the old gods had left the earth, and with it, the woman who had carried that power for so many centuries.

Don't miss out!

Visit the website below and you can sign up to receive emails whenever Catherine J Rosser publishes a new book. There's no charge and no obligation.

https://books2read.com/r/B-A-FGQOC-NVYDF

BOOKS 2 READ

Connecting independent readers to independent writers.

Did you love *The Eternal Circle*? Then you should read *The Thistle Queen*[1] by Catherine J Rosser!

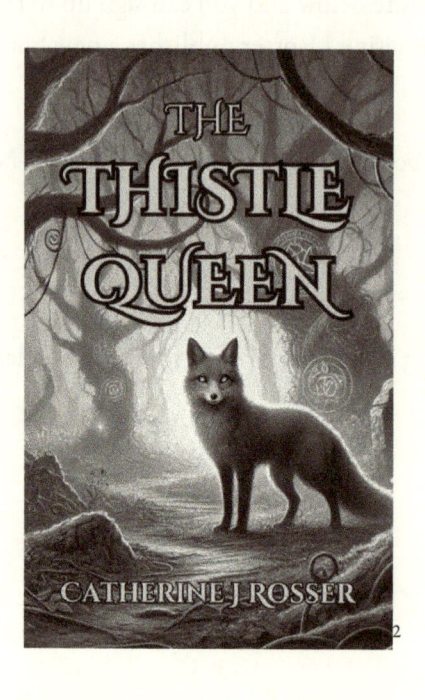

In the cursed forest of Thrysseldown, where shadows whisper and thorns grow thicker than hope, the Thistle Queen reigns. Once a guardian of the land, her heart was corrupted by forbidden love and betrayal, casting an ancient curse that turned the forest into a realm of twisted magic. Now, the forest thrives on fear, its paths shifting and dark creatures lurking in every shadow.

Elowen, a humble gardener with an extraordinary connection to the earth, stumbles upon a long-forgotten

---

1. https://books2read.com/u/bayO1L

2. https://books2read.com/u/bayO1L

secret—the truth of the Thistle Queen's curse. Alongside Rook, a roguish thief with a haunted past, and Periwinkle, a cursed fae prince in the form of a fox, Elowen embarks on a perilous quest to restore the forest and free its people from the Queen's relentless grasp.

As they journey deeper into the heart of Thrysseldown, battling ancient magic and facing their darkest fears, they unravel the tragic history of the Queen and her once-sacred bond to the forest. But breaking the curse comes with a price, and not everyone will survive the trials of the forest. In a land where light and darkness blur, and sacrifice is inevitable, Elowen must decide how far she is willing to go to restore balance and confront the Queen who was once the forest's savior.

The Thistle Queen is a dark fairytale of magic, sacrifice, and redemption, set in a world where the forest holds its own secrets, and even the deepest love can turn to ruin.

Read more at https://catherinejrosser.com/.

Also by Catherine J Rosser

The Eternal Magic Series
The Magic Within

The Isles of Fate Series
The Crimson Raven: A Tale of Captain Poppie O'Malley
The Siren's Call: A Tale of Love and Treachery on the High Seas
Winds of Fortune

The Keeper of Ages
The Eternal Circle

Standalone
Beyond the Horizon
Echoes in the Abyss
Haven Falls

The Fractured Mind
The Next Chapter: Embracing Midlife with Purpose, Peace, and Possibility
The Thistle Queen
Dream Interpretation: A Journey Through the Mind's Mirror

Watch for more at https://catherinejrosser.com/.

About the Author

Catherine J. Rosser is a fantasy author who weaves together myth, magic, and unforgettable journeys. Known for her vivid storytelling and rich characters, she brings epic worlds to life with themes of destiny and self-discovery. When not writing, Catherine draws inspiration from nature, channeling its beauty into her imaginative tales.

Read more at https://catherinejrosser.com/.